Keyhles

Modern parables of faith, identity, purpose, and belonging.

STEVEN L. BARR

For my Disney Cast Member family around the world—
whose photos hang on my office wall beside me, and
whose lives continue to shape my own.

You are more than a costume or a nametag.
You are stories in motion, written by God's own hand—
filled with hope, struggle, kindness, and quiet courage.

This is for you—
for the way you've shown up, for the way you've cared,
for the way you've made others feel seen.

You are the reason I write these stories.

Contents

HOW TO READ THIS BOOK

There's no right or wrong way to read Keyholes.

You can begin at the beginning or jump to the middle. You can read the stories or skip around and see what catches your attention.

The only caution I'd give is this: don't read too many parables at once. These stories are meant to linger, to marinate in your heart and mind. Hold them in your heart for a while. There's no need to rush through this book.

Each parable stands on its own, and yet, taken together, they reveal a bigger story. A story you're already part of, even if you don't realize it yet.

Parables are like mini-movies for the imagination. They transport you briefly but powerfully into another world. Sometimes, that world feels familiar, anchored in everyday life. Other times, it exists in a space between reality and imagination, where truth can slip past what feels ordinary and reach deeper places within you.

You see with someone else's eyes, feel with someone else's heart, and walk in someone else's shoes.

They don't just inform you; they form you. They soften your defenses, stir your empathy, and sneak past your usual filters.

Parables are not puzzles to be solved. They are mirrors, windows, and yes, keyholes—small openings that invite you to lean in, slow down, and look more closely.

They're not always clear at first. In fact, some may confuse you. Others might make you feel a bit uncomfortable.

That's okay.

Even as the author of these parables, a few of them rub me the wrong way. Yet I've discovered that holding space for the tension, instead of dismissing it, often leads me to a deeper truth in the story.

If you feel something stirring within you, pause.
If something bothers you, read it again.
Sit with it for a while.
Ask why.

The discomfort may point to something deeper.

And when a parable resonates?
Let it echo.
Let it shape you.

Some stories will feel obvious. Others will feel hidden, like they're whispering something just out of reach. Don't worry. The companion videos will offer a bit more clarity, but don't rush there too quickly.

Trust the process.
The story is doing more than you know.

UNLOCKING THE STORY BEHIND THE STORY

At the end of each parable in KEYHOLES, you'll notice a small black-and-white square. This is called a QR code—short for Quick Response code. It works like a digital key.

When you scan a QR code using your phone or tablet, it will instantly open a short 2–3 minute video where I personally unpack the meaning of that parable. These videos are simple, thoughtful reflections to help you take the story deeper into your life, your questions, and your heart.

1. Open your phone's camera. Most smartphones (iPhones and Android phones) will automatically recognize a QR code using the regular camera.

2. Point the camera at the QR code. You don't need to take a picture. Just hold your phone steady so the code is centered in the frame.

3. After a moment, a link should pop up on your screen. Tap it, and it will take you to the video.

TIP: If nothing appears, check your phone settings to make sure QR code scanning is turned on. Alternatively, you can download a free "QR Code Reader" app from your phone's app store.

What You'll Find in the Videos:

These aren't lectures or sermons.
They're quiet conversations.
Moments to pause and reflect.

Sometimes I'll ask you a question. Other times I'll simply help you see the story in a new light.

My hope is that each video helps you take one small step forward toward clarity, healing, hope, and ultimately, toward Jesus.

A LITTLE BIT ABOUT ME

I love Jesus.

But I don't fit the description most people imagine when they hear me say that I love Jesus—especially in many church circles.

I've spent most of my life questioning assumptions, challenging man-made systems, and disrupting the status quo. For me, asking why or why not has always come as naturally as breathing.

I thrive in a space somewhere between Kingdom reality and holy imagination. Pictures, parables, and principles are the languages of my soul. That's how I understand Jesus and how I talk about Him with people who suspect anything having to do with faith.

I mentor Disney Cast Members[1] worldwide, walking with them through life, faith, and purpose, not from a platform, but side by side, as a friend. I listen—really listen—until their stories resonate with the subtle echoes of grace, and I can hear how God is gently revealing Himself in the rhythms of their everyday lives.

You could say I'm planting Jesus, scattering seeds of His love, truth, compassion, and grace through the sacred work of relationship.

---

1. All employees who work for The Walt Disney Company worldwide.

More than anything, I'm a storyteller.

Not the kind which end with tidy answers wrapped in a bow. I like to tell stories that cause others to look at life from a different perspective, to spark their curiosity, and open their imaginations to the possibilities of something more.

This book is a collection of some of those stories.

I hope it awakens something within you; a memory you can't name, a longing you've always felt, a glimpse of something that you've been searching for your whole life...

...maybe without ever realizing it was looking for you.

INTRODUCTION

Most people miss it.

Not because it's far away, but because it's so close.
Not because it's silent, but because it whispers.

The Kingdom of Heaven is a hidden world woven into this one.
A secret in plain sight, waiting with anticipation to be revealed.

It doesn't shout.
It doesn't dazzle.
It doesn't demand to be noticed.

It waits for those willing to pause, to look closely and listen even closer.

Jesus was the most effective communicator ever.
But he didn't speak like most church leaders do today.

He didn't distribute outlines or deliver big-screen presentations filled with bullet points. He didn't create academic frameworks or impress with theological acrobatics. He didn't teach from a curriculum filled with pathways and processes.

Jesus told stories.
Simple, surprising, subversive stories.

They weren't doors, wide open and obvious. They were keyholes; parables, principles, paradoxes, and patterns.

With many stories like these, he presented his message to them, fitting the stories to their experience and maturity. He was never without a story when he spoke. - Mark 4:34a (MSG)

This was his way, not just to explain, but to reveal. Not to satisfy curiosity, but to awaken it.

But His stories didn't always make sense to everyone.

To the proud, like the religious elite, they stirred up clouds of confusion. To the humble, those honestly seeking, they became windows of clarity.

The parables tested more than intellect; they tested the posture of the heart.

Each story was a keyhole through which we could glimpse the Kingdom, in small, subtle, yet profoundly disruptive ways.

This was the paradox of Jesus: He hid the sacred in the ordinary, not to keep it secret, but to see who would look for it.

Today, we continue to find comfort, captivation, and challenge in Jesus' use of creative simplicity to reveal who He is and what His Kingdom is all about. We remain in awe of His ability to present the infinite mysteries of Heaven in ways that anyone, even a child—or perhaps a child at heart—could understand.

"The Kingdom of Heaven is like..." – Jesus

Whether highlighting a pearl of great worth, a lost coin, a rebellious son, a wandering sheep, or even a flower blooming in the field, Jesus crafted an image of His Kingdom that anyone could see, hear, smell, touch, and taste with their imagination.

But seeing through a keyhole isn't automatic. It takes more than a perspective. It takes a posture.

You have to slow down, fine-tune your focus, and position your heart to receive.

That's why Jesus said, "*Listen.*"

He often finished a story by saying, "*For those who have ears, let them hear.*" He invited, even challenged, the listener to engage with their heart to truly grasp the simple yet eternally profound wisdom He was revealing.

For those with ears to hear today, these eternal echoes still awaken something within us.

For those with eyes to see, the view through those keyholes becomes more vivid and vibrant each time we look through them.

This book is my attempt to follow Jesus' rhythm, not with lengthy explanations or complicated theology, but through keyholes.

Each one revealing a glimpse of the power and wonder of time-less truth.

So, pause. Take a deep breath. Look and listen closely. Not just with your eyes and ears.

But most importantly, with your heart.

THE ANTIQUE COMPASS

"Everyone should follow their truth."

It's a phrase that sounds tolerant, open-minded, even thoughtful. But what happens when everyone insists their direction is right, even as they drift farther and farther apart? In a world where truth is a matter of opinion, how can we know if anything can be trusted at all? But if truth really exists, wouldn't it be the one thing that doesn't change, no matter which way we're facing?

"Then you will know the truth and the truth will set you free."

- (Jesus) John 8:32 (NIV)

The small group gathered in a circle, each clutching a blank map.

They were given one instruction for the quest: "*Trust your truth.*"

Beyond the circle, a mist-thick forest waited—silent, endless, hiding something they all wanted. Not gold or jewels, but a treasure of worth beyond counting—*significance, meaning, acceptance.* The very things every heart longs for.

The maps offered only one instruction: "*Follow what feels right for you.*" No landmarks. No directions. Only a clean sheet and a confident promise.

A dozen searchers stepped into the woods, each one certain that their inner truth would lead them to the prize. Some followed the wind. Some followed the birds. A few followed their horoscopes.

She tried to follow her heart, but it changed direction daily. Some mornings, it whispered hope. Some nights, it thundered fear. At dawn it swore she was close; by dusk it warned she'd never arrive.

The farther they went, the more tangled the paths . Lost and laughing, they crossed trails again and again. Soon they argued over which way to go—confusion clashing with false confidence.

A man declared he'd found the way. He built a wooden platform to announce it, and a crowd followed him with cheers—only to end up in thorns or walking in circles for days.

Frustration grew. Anger followed. No one wanted to admit they were lost. Some doubled down; others pretended they'd found the treasure just to save face.

One evening, a heavy fog rolled in. It didn't just surround her; it seeped inside her, dimming the voice she had trusted. Her map was smudged and soaked. Her certainty was threadbare. Her steps dragged as if the earth itself resisted her. Her heart—the guide she was told to trust—had gone strangely silent.

At last, she collapsed beneath an ancient tree. Her body was weary. Her soul, more so.

That's when she saw it: a faint glow flickering far ahead. Through the mist appeared a small cabin—wooden, weathered by time. Smoke curled from a crooked chimney. A window glimmered gold and orange behind the curtains.

Drawn by the warmth, she climbed the porch steps. The door stood ajar, as if it had been waiting for her all along. She hesitated, then crossed the threshold.

"Hello?" Her voice was barely above a whisper.

A mature voice, warm as the firelight, floated from within. "Come in. I've been expecting you."

Inside, the room smelled of pine and tea leaves. A fire crackled in the hearth. Shelves lined the walls, stacked with books and strange instruments.

An old man sat in a wingback chair, reading a book that looked older than time itself. When he saw her, he closed it gently and studied her face as if he already knew her.

"You're lost," he said—his voice kind enough to make denial impossible.

She nearly protested but found no words. He gestured to the empty chair across from him.

"Sit. You've been wandering out there for a long time."

She sank into the chair. He handed her a steaming cup of tea. It tasted exactly as she liked it, though she hadn't told him a thing.

Lowering her voice, she confessed, "*I was told to follow my truth.*"

He nodded slowly. "*And how has that gone?*"

She looked down at her scratched hands, her bruised arms, and her worn-out shoes. Her silence answered for her.

"*It's all right,*" he added gently. "*You're not the first to come through my door.*"

He rose and walked to a shelf, drawing down a small wooden box. From it he took a round, weathered compass—simple and surprisingly heavy, its brass cool against her palm.

"*This doesn't point north,*" he said. "*It points to the One who made it.*"

She traced the needle with her thumb. For the first time in days, something felt steady.

A smirk tugged at her mouth as she turned the compass over. "*It's old. Does it still work?*"

His hand rested over it like a blessing. "*It's never failed.*"

She looked at the needle again, then back at him. "*What if someone else's compass says something different?*"

He smiled, eyes kind. "*Then one of you is wrong.*"

Turning to the fire, he stoked it with a rod. Sparks leapt up the chimney. "*Truth doesn't change to make us feel better.*" He stared into the flames. "*If it changed, you'd still be wandering the woods.*"

She held the compass tightly. The needle stayed true.

"Why doesn't everyone use one of these?" she asked.

He pointed gently to her heart. "Because it won't let you pretend. It won't let you be your own guide. Most would rather be lost on their own terms than found on someone else's."

For a long while, neither spoke. The fire crackled as if it understood. She felt the puzzle pieces of her life beginning to fall into place.

When she rose to leave, she tucked the compass into her coat and thanked the old man. Stepping back into the dark, she felt lighter than when she'd entered. Not tired. Not confused. Light.

She told no one of her choice to follow the compass. She didn't need to—the change was visible.

Some saw her new direction and laughed. She didn't mind. Others shook their heads in disapproval. A few shouted after her, "You're giving up your freedom!"

She chose not to argue. Her feet felt steady now. The path was still steep in places, still shadowed in others, but it no longer shifted beneath her.

She had a direction that didn't sway with her moods. A truth—not born in her heart, yet able at last to lead it home.

And as she disappeared into the thinning fog, she began to believe, compelled to know this truth.

Because—if the old man was right—this truth already knew her.

THE BACKPACK AND THE ROPE

Why is it so hard to let go—especially when holding on is hurting us? We often cling to what we've earned, built, or believe defines us, even when it weighs us down. The idea of surrender can feel like weakness or failure, especially in a culture that celebrates self-sufficiency. But what if the very thing we resist—the letting go—is the first step toward real freedom? What if rescue isn't about proving ourselves, but about accepting a kind of help that humbles us... and heals us?

"I am the way and the truth and the life. No one comes to the Father except through me."

-Jesus (John 14:6) NIV

Silence.

It was an eerie quiet that follows a fall—heavy, breath-holding—broken only by the sound of labored breathing and the wind.

The hiker had taken one step too many. Or so he thought.

One moment he was steady on the narrow trail; the next, the earth crumbled beneath his boot. It happened in an instant—just a gasp, a blur—and gravity claimed him. Rocks scraped past as branches snapped. His body, no longer his own, was at the mercy of the mountain.

The truth was more painful than the unstable rock. It wasn't the trail that failed. It was the weight of his pack—top-of-the-line, filled with climbing clips, high-tech tools, dried meals for a week, a weather-stained journal, and medals dulled by old scratches from past climbs. Each item carried meaning. Each piece, a symbol of success and self-sufficiency.

With every mile, the heavy pack had become more burdensome, pulling him off-balance until a gust of wind sent him tumbling.

Now he sat, bloodied and bruised, stranded on a narrow ledge carved into the stony face of the mountain. Beneath him, a drop too far; above him, a climb too steep. The wind mocked with each gust, whispering he wouldn't last the night.

Word of his fall reached the rescue base below. A team arrived on the ridge above, calling down to him.

"We see you! We're sending the rope!"

A thick, weather-worn line unfurled into view—knotted, anchored, tested. It swayed in the wind as if beckoning him to trust. But he hesitated.

"This is it?" he shouted upward. "Just... a rope?"

"Yes!" came the reply. "It's secure. We've used it many times before. You need to trust us!"

He stared at the rope. The longer he looked, the more discomfort grew. Just one rope? One way? Surely there were other options—dignified ones, cleaner ones, something that didn't feel like surrender.

He imagined a helicopter lowering a harness or a hidden path around the mountain—something that made sense. Instead, a single rope asking him to trust what he couldn't control. It felt almost offensive.

He glanced at the pack beside him. Most of it was still intact. There was incalculable value in that gear—the tools he trusted, the things that defined him. To leave it behind felt like erasing himself.

"Can I climb up with my gear?" he called out.

There was a pause, then the voice above: "No. The rope is strong, but the way up is narrow—too narrow for the backpack. You'll have to leave it behind."

"But this gear... it's part of me. I can't just let it go."

"You have to," the rescuer yelled back. "It's what pulled you down in the first place."

The wind bit deeper into his clothes as he sat in silence. To grab the rope meant admitting he couldn't save himself. This wasn't how it was supposed to go. He had planned every detail, studied the routes, prepared for anything—except this.

Except needing help.

"*I'm not helpless,*" he muttered, teeth clenched. "*I've trained for this. I've climbed harder cliffs than this. I just need to think it through.*"

His eyes returned to the backpack. For the first time, he noticed how it sagged—not just from weight but from years of wear. Frayed seams, cracked buckles, the faint smell of sweat and old fear. It represented every mountain climbed, every battle fought, every scar earned along the way. The backpack wasn't an accessory; it was his identity.

A loose stone skidded beneath his heel. He caught his balance—barely. The ledge was becoming unstable, with small fragments crumbling away into the abyss. The ground beneath him was a countdown. The rope drifted closer in the wind. Rescue was at hand. But without the backpack, it would feel like climbing naked.

Tears burned his eyes, though he didn't know why—anger, embarrassment, wounded pride, all tangled together. This rescue felt exposing. He sat frozen by indecision—half-turned, half-torn, completely terrified.

The ledge shifted again, larger chunks of rock breaking loose. The backpack would soon slip away with the crumbling ledge. His eyes darted between rope and pack; his chest tightened; shock began to seize his limbs.

Leaving the backpack would cost him everything.

Maybe... he thought desperately, *maybe I can figure out another way. I just need a little more time.*

But the mountain gave him none. A crack split beneath his feet, racing toward the edge. Dust burst upward as the rock gave way. In a heartbeat, the ledge was collapsing—the rope swinging close, the backpack sliding toward the void.

He had only a heartbeat to decide...

... the backpack or the rope.

THE UNEXPECTED VISIT

We can often go to great lengths to be noticed, admired, or chosen. We polish ourselves, curate our image, try to say the right things, do the right things—hoping it will be enough. But deep down, many of us still wonder if we're missing something. Could it be that what really matters isn't how impressive we look, but how honest we're willing to be? And could it be that what we long for—love—is attracted not to our best performance, but to our truest self?

God judges persons differently than humans do. Men and women look at the face; God looks into the heart.

-1 Samuel 16:7b (MSG)

Word spread like wildfire: the King was coming.

The whole town buzzed with excitement.

The announcement declared he would choose one home to visit and share a meal. Everyone imagined what it might be like to be the chosen ones. They knew this could be their moment to shine.

They sprang into action.

Sidewalks were scrubbed, lawns trimmed, and fences painted. Front doors were brightened with a fresh coat of color. Banners were strung and yard signs posted.

Some residents placed bumper stickers with the King's crest on their cars. Others framed his sayings and mounted them on their walls. Songs were composed. Parades planned. Speeches rehearsed.

Every family prepared what they would say when he came to their door:

"Your Highness, everything is ready."
"We have done all this for you."
"We have spared no effort or expense to honor your name."

To ensure nothing spoiled the view, the townspeople built a massive berm of earth around the outskirts—high enough to hide what they wished he'd never see—the garbage dump, the weather-worn houses near the sewage plant, every eyesore beyond the city's edge. They wanted the King to witness only their finest.

As the day drew near, they admired their work and congratulated one another. They were confident that the King would be grateful. They were certain he would be impressed with all of their effort.

And then they waited...

...and waited...

...and waited.

But the King never came.

No limousines rolled through the pristine streets—no royal procession, no parade—only silence.

Days stretched into weeks. Excitement gave way to confusion. Confusion hardened into frustration.

"We did all this for nothing?"
"What was the point of our preparation?"
"He must've known how hard we worked."

Then a whisper rippled through the town: the King had come.

But he never entered the city. He didn't walk their polished sidewalks or knock on their decorated doors. Instead, he remained beyond the berm—the very places they had worked so hard to hide.

He had visited a dilapidated shack with a rusted tin roof and a porch that leaned as if it might collapse. There, he spent the evening with an elderly widow.

She had lived alone most of her life—unnoticed, forgotten. A nobody in the eyes of the town. She had no family, no reputation, and no legacy. Her only income came from selling apples from a twisted old tree in her yard. Even among her few neighbors, she was overlooked.

When she heard the knock, she hesitated. She was not used to having visitors at her door. She wasn't accustomed to being noticed at all.

"Surely it couldn't be him... not here, not for me."

She hadn't prepared a thing. No banner. No feast. Not even a clean room to offer. Her hands were stained from working in the soil. Her dress had worn thin. She felt embarrassed—regardless of who was knocking.

And yet, when she cracked open the door and saw the King standing there, she gasped.

Every instinct told her to explain, to apologize, to hide. But he just smiled and introduced himself. He called her by name. He told her that his reason for coming was to spend the evening with her.

Without thinking, she threw open the door and cast her frail arms around him.

No proper manners, no polished greeting, no rehearsed speech—just joy: unfiltered, unrestrained, and unpolished.

She welcomed him in. Her laughter turned to tears—raw, unfiltered, unstoppable. It wasn't just joy. It was something deeper—a secret hope buried so long ago she'd forgotten it existed.

She never expected him to come. Not to her. Not to someone so insignificant and unworthy.

They talked for hours. She became so absorbed in the conversation that she completely forgot to offer him anything to eat. She had nothing to give—no set table, no prepared food, and no quotes on the wall—only her gratitude and her amazement that he would choose to be with her.

As the evening drew to a close, the King embraced her with affection, as if she were family herself. Then he placed a letter in her trembling hands, sealed with his royal mark.

It was a permanent open invitation. She could visit him anytime she wished.

Tears blurred her vision as she reached the last line of the letter—six simple words, written in his own hand:

"*I am always here for you.*"

When the news of the King's unexpected visit reached the city leaders, they were indignant.

"*That woman made no preparations!*" the mayor fumed.
"*Her home had no spirit of excellence!*" a councilman snapped.
"*Why would he visit someone with nothing to offer?*" another demanded.

The leaders sent a formal letter to the palace:

"*We made the city immaculate for you, yet you visited one who hadn't prepared. We honored your image in every street and square, yet you shunned us with your absence. We labored to make our homes worthy—polishing, setting every table—only to hear you sat with one who offered nothing. After all we did, why waste your presence on them?*"

A week later, a letter arrived bearing the King's seal. Inside was the short response, written in the King's own hand:

You offered me a show.
She gave me something real—a humble heart.
That's all I was looking for.

THE RAINCOATS

Sometimes life hands us things that don't seem to fit—roles we didn't choose, responsibilities that feel too heavy or too small, moments that leave us exposed or misunderstood. We resist them, question them, try to make sense of why we're the ones carrying what feels awkward or unfair. But what if those ill-fitting moments weren't mistakes? What if someone else was meant to benefit from them?

Put yourself aside, and help others get ahead. Don't be obsessed with getting your own advantage. Forget yourselves long enough to lend a helping hand.

- Philippians 2:4 (MSG)

The morning was rain-soaked and gray.

Clouds sagged low, heavy with silence, and the streets shimmered with puddles.

A mother stood by the front door holding a bright yellow raincoat. She extended it to her son, who eyed it with obvious disapproval.

The coat was far too large for his small frame—the sleeves drooped well past his wrists, and the hem nearly skimmed the ground.

He pulled it on reluctantly, his mouth twisting with complaint.

"I look *ridiculous*," he mumbled under his breath.

With his head down, he stepped outside, hoping the neighbors wouldn't see him—or the absurd coat.

As he trudged down the slick sidewalk, he noticed an elderly man standing alone in the pouring rain. He was leaning heavily on a weathered cane. His clothes were drenched. No coat, no umbrella—nothing to shield him from the downpour. He looked fragile, like a brittle tree waiting for the next gust to snap it.

The boy's first instinct was to look away, keep walking, and stay dry.

The raincoat was his, even if it didn't fit right.

But something stirred in him—a quiet, persistent tug.

He hesitated, then sighed. Slowly, he slipped off the oversized coat and walked toward the man. Without a word, he draped it over the man's shoulders.

To his surprise, it fit him perfectly. The man's thin frame disappeared beneath its warmth and shelter.

He nodded a silent thanks, and the boy turned and walked home, soaked to the bone.

When he arrived, dripping and shivering, his mother opened the door without a word. She looked at him—soaked, empty-handed—and said nothing. She simply took his wet clothes and placed them near the heater, her silence speaking more than words.

A few weeks later, the rain returned. It came with wind this time, rattling windows and drumming on rooftops.

The boy's mother handed him another coat, one that was far too small. The sleeves stopped above his wrists, the buttons barely fastened, and the fabric pulled tight across his chest.

He could feel the frustration within him beginning to boil.

"*Seriously? This again?*" he grumbled to himself.

But something in his mother's eyes silenced him before he spoke a word. She wasn't cruel. She wasn't careless. She was—he realized—intentional.

Once again, he stepped into the storm.

Further down the flooded street, he spotted a little girl huddled against a stone wall, trembling. Her clothes clung to her skin and her teeth chattered.

He stood still for a moment, torn. The coat barely covered him—how could it cover her?

But the tug came again, stronger than his frustration. Gritting his teeth, he unfastened the coat and gently wrapped it around the little girl's shoulders.

The change was instant—the coat swallowed her, but in the best way.

She gave him a shy smile, then turned and disappeared down the alley.

He walked home drenched once more. And again, his mother said nothing.

More time passed, and with it, more storms.

On the third occasion, the rain came sideways, driven by an icy wind.

The boy's mother handed him a coat that was stiff and rough, scratching his arms and boxing him in like armor he didn't choose.

This time he was angry.

"Why do I always get the ones that never fit?"

But the storm wouldn't wait, and neither did the strange pull in his chest.

Reluctantly, he stepped outside.

Halfway down the block, he saw him—a boy from school crouched on the curb, shielding his torn backpack from the rain.

He was the boy who laughed too loudly in the cafeteria and pushed others in the hall—the kind who never missed a chance to mock a coat like this.

The boy hesitated. He could hear it already: the sneers, the sideways looks, the jokes whispered just loud enough for him to hear.

"Look at him. He looks like a wooden soldier."

He almost walked away. Almost.

But something fierce and wordless stirred inside him. With trembling hands, he peeled off the stiff, miserable coat and held it out.

The other boy snatched it with a smirk, turned without a word, and walked away.

The coat fit him.

Shivering, heart aching, the boy walked home—angry, tired, undone.

When he stepped through the front door, his mother simply opened her arms.

She asked no questions, offered no lectures. Only a quiet presence.

And the pattern continued.

Each time the rain returned, his mother handed him another coat.

It was always too big, too small, too stiff, or too thin.

Every time, it made him uncomfortable. Every time, he encountered someone who needed it more. And every time, the coat fit them better.

One day, weary from yet another storm, he came home coatless and soaked again. Water ran from his sleeves, and tears stung his eyes.

He stood in the doorway, fists clenched, shoulders slumped.

"Why do you keep giving me coats that don't fit? They make me look ridiculous... and I always end up wet and cold."

His mother knelt in front of him. She took his numb hands in hers and looked at him—really looked at him. Her eyes were tender with compassion.

"My darling, you don't understand," she said gently. "The coats fit perfectly every time."

She reached up and brushed a tear from his cheek.

"They were never yours to keep. They were meant to bless someone else...

...and you helped make that happen."

THE GIRL ON THE BACK ROW

Sometimes we can be cruel—not with fists, but with silence, with glances, with words we whisper behind cupped hands. Words that remind someone they don't belong. We judge them before knowing their story. We expect them to act like insiders while they're still standing on the threshold, unsure if they're even welcome. This story is about longing. It's about someone brave enough to come back to a place that once wounded them, and a quiet moment of grace that reminds us all: when someone is searching, the last thing they need is condemnation. What they need is space... and love.

"Don't pick on people, jump on their failures, criticize their faults—unless, of course, you want the same treatment. That critical spirit has a way of boomeranging."

- (Jesus) Matthew 7:1,2 (MSG)

She slipped into the church late—on purpose. The music had already begun, loud enough to mask the click of the closing door but not enough to keep people from noticing. They always noticed. Not just her timing. Her.

She used to come here—used to sing on that stage and ask the hard questions in youth group, the ones that made leaders shift in their folding chairs and glance at one another, desperate for an easy way out.

"Well... that's complicated, sweetie."
"It's just a phase. It'll pass."
"You should pray about it."

On weekend retreats she would lie in her sleeping bag beneath the stars, whispering her questions to God. Did He see her? Did He like what He saw? Back then, she believed this was where she'd find her answers—until she came out. Not with a megaphone. Not online. Just a quiet confession to her small-group leader, someone she thought was safe.

Word spread anyway. Fast—at the speed of a message ping. Suddenly, she no longer belonged.

Now she pulled her coat tight, though the sanctuary was warm and her palms were already damp. The coat made her feel smaller, almost invisible—safer. A well-dressed usher near the aisle caught her eye. He smiled—only with his mouth—and pointed her toward the back.

Last row. End seat. As far from the front as she could sit without being in the parking lot.

When she sat down, a few heads turned. Two teenage girls, two rows ahead, peeked over their shoulders and whispered behind cupped hands. A giggle slipped out. She didn't need to guess. She knew their kind. She used to be their kind.

"... isn't she the one who came out junior year?"
"... always asking why God made her that way."
"... moved in with her girlfriend, right?"
"... her parents must be crushed."
"... she doesn't hide it very well."

She fixed her eyes on the lyrics glowing on the screen, mouthing the chorus about mercy though the words blurred—not from tears but from exhaustion, the kind that clings to the bones and makes you forget how to breathe. She hadn't come to make a statement, not to stir the pot or defy expectations. She was just... here. Drawn by something she couldn't name, drawn the way you catch the scent of something familiar—like home, even if home never felt safe.

The pastor took the stage. Still the same clean-cut smile, the same easy charm—like a toothpaste ad holding a Bible. He cracked a few jokes. The crowd laughed. Everyone seemed at ease. Well... almost everyone.

His sermon was on the prodigal son. Of course it was. She could have preached it herself: the son who demands his inheritance, spends it all on reckless living, ends up feeding pigs just to survive, crawls back home rehearsing his apology. The father runs to meet him—arms wide, no questions asked. Everyone loves the running part. No one talks much about the older brother—standing on the porch, arms crossed, refusing to step inside.

She shifted in her seat. She wasn't sure which one she was—the runaway or the one left standing outside. All she knew was this: she was a story no one wanted to tell.

Halfway through the message she considered slipping out—before the predictable altar call, before the polite small talk, *before someone decided to speak the truth in love.* She reached for her coat.

That's when she felt it—a hand. Soft. Wrinkled. Resting gently over hers. Startled, she turned.

An elderly woman sat beside her—how had she missed her? Snow-white hair, a faded floral blouse, a small cane leaning against the pew. Her eyes were gentle but keen. She leaned close, her voice just above a whisper.

"I'm so glad you're here."

The girl blinked, unsure how to respond.

"I've been praying someone would sit here again," the woman whispered.

The girl managed a faint smile—more politeness than belief. The woman's hand gave a gentle squeeze.

"My daughter used to sit right here. Long time ago. She left angry. Thought Jesus didn't want her anymore. But He did. He always did. These people here... they don't aways know how to show it."

The girl swallowed hard. The woman's voice stayed warm, steady.

"I don't know your story, dear," she said, her voice tender, almost like a lullaby. *"But I can tell you this..."*

She kept her gaze on the front of the room as she added, *"I've sat in this row more Sundays than I can count. I've seen saints. I've seen sinners..."*

She paused, a small smile tugging at her lips as if recalling a memory. *"... and I've seen the ones who no longer know who they are anymore."*

Then she turned toward the girl. "And some of the most honest worship I've ever heard came from people who barely whispered."

The girl looked back at her—this woman didn't flinch. Didn't frown. Didn't scan her clothes or her posture or her past. She simply stayed—present, understanding, safe.

Soft music played as the pastor prayed. A few went forward for prayer, a few slipped out the back, but most stayed seated with heads bowed.

The girl stayed too. Not because she was afraid, but because — for the first time in years — she didn't feel the need to run away.

THE WATER BOTTLE

Some things look ordinary but hold extraordinary potential. A gift. A promise. A rescue. But we often hesitate to receive what we don't understand. So instead, we carry it—close enough to feel safe, but never close enough to let it in. We guard what was meant to heal. We wait for the perfect moment to trust. And sometimes... we wait too long.

"Anyone who drinks the water I give will never thirst—not ever. The water I give will be an artesian spring within, gushing fountains of endless life."

- (Jesus) John 4:14 (MSG)

He found the bottle resting on a worn-out park bench, half-hidden behind a newspaper that had fluttered there days ago. At first, he didn't think much of it—just another stray item left behind in a city where things were constantly coming and going.

But something about this bottle made him stop. It was perfectly sealed—clear and cool to the touch despite the warm air. Light danced through the water inside in a way he couldn't explain. It shimmered, not like plastic or glass but like something alive—something waiting.

And though it bore no label or markings, it seemed as if it had been placed there...

... just for him.

He looked around. No one was nearby. No sign of who might have left it. A part of him hesitated—maybe it was too strange, too good to be safe. But another part, deeper and quieter, told him this was not a mistake. He was sure this bottle was more than just water—that somehow, it held something meant for him.

He picked it up. It was heavier than it looked—not physically, but in significance. He couldn't explain it. The bottle felt important. Intimate. As if it were a message, a gift, or a promise.

He slipped it into his bag and carried it home.

That night, he placed it on the table beside his bed. The condensation had faded, but the glow remained—subtle, like a candle still flickering as the wind passes by. He sat on the edge of the bed and stared at it. There was no voice. No writing in the sky. But the silence around the bottle spoke louder than anything in his life.

It wasn't waiting for him to be ready—it was inviting him to respond. Not someday. Now.

But he hesitated, caught between the hope it offered and the doubt he couldn't silence.

Days passed.
Then weeks.

He began carrying the bottle with him wherever he went—not to drink it, but to keep it close. It sat beside his keyboard at work. Rode with him in the passenger seat. Rested on his lap during long, quiet drives.

People noticed it.

"What's with the bottle?" they'd ask.

He never had a simple answer.

"It's kind of special," he'd say, or sometimes, "It's just something I'm holding on to."

But deep down, he knew what they didn't. The bottle wasn't just water. It was hope. Security. A kind of sacred backup plan. He liked knowing it was there. He liked how it made him feel—like he wasn't entirely alone.

There were moments—long nights, aching questions, sleepless spirals—when he came close to opening it. He'd reach out, hands trembling, fingers brushing the cap.

But each time, his hesitation would whisper:

"What if I open it and nothing happens?"
"What if I waste it?"
"What if I'm not ready?"

He wanted to believe it was real. But he was more afraid of being disappointed than he was of being thirsty.

He waited.

He became oddly proud of his patience—proud of carrying it with him every day, proud of being "open to it," even if he'd never taken a sip.

Then came the day everything fell apart.

He lost his job. He missed his train. He fought with someone he loved. The pressure in his chest had built all day, like a steel band tightening around his ribcage. He needed to get out—needed air.

The world began spinning faster and faster around him. The pain in his chest became excruciating.

He collapsed on a crumbling sidewalk—trembling, dimming, parched.

There in his hand—miraculously—was the bottle, full and un-opened.

A stranger saw him fall and rushed over to help; a young woman, out of breath. She saw the bottle.

"*Drink it! Please!*" she pleaded, reaching toward it.

But he pulled it back to his chest.

His cracked lips moved slowly, his voice barely audible.

"No... *not yet. It's mine. I'm saving it. I'm—waiting... I'm—waiting... I'm—*"

His mouth tried to form the words, but no breath came to carry them. His eyes fluttered. His grip loosened. The bottle slipped from his fingers and rolled onto the concrete.

The woman knelt there beside him, weeping over his still body.

The bottle was still there—untouched, glowing in the evening light, its seal unbroken.

Still able to satisfy...

... still able to save.

THE ENDLESS PARADE

We live in a world obsessed with what's next—new trends, viral movements, and flashy ideas that promise a better life if we just keep up. But beneath the surface of our constant chasing is a deeper ache for something lasting. Are we chasing something real, or just running with the crowd?

"Are you tired? Worn out? Burned out on religion? Come to me. Get away with me and you'll recover your life. I'll show you how to take a real rest. Walk with me and work with me—watch how I do it. Learned the unforced rhythms of grace. I won't lay anything heavy or ill-fitting on you. Keep company with me and you'll learn to live freely and lightly."

-(Jesus) Matthew 11:28-30 (MSG)

It started with a sound—soft at first, like distant drumming. It echoed through alleyways and bounced off glass towers until the entire city seemed to vibrate with it.

People paused. Heads turned. Screens dimmed. Someone stepped out of a café. Someone else pointed down the street and shouted, "Here comes the parade!" That was all it took. Feet moved. Phones rose. The ripple became a current, and the current became a crowd.

Then it arrived—louder than expected, brighter than it should've been. The first float came into view, towering and gold-draped, flashing bold letters from every side:

LOOK GOOD. FEEL POWERFUL.

Music blared through the speakers, pounding like a heartbeat too fast to relax. People applauded. Some climbed onto benches for a better view.

The next float rolled up—sleeker and faster than the first. High-def screens curved around its sides, shimmering with shifting colors. The message glided across in smooth, animated text:

YOU DESERVE THE BEST.

Images of sports cars, big houses, and fine dining drew eyes, nodded heads, and stirred quiet cravings.

Then another appeared:

FIND 1,000 FOLLOWERS IN FIVE EASY STEPS.

Each float was flashier than the last. One promised overnight success. Another offered instant identity—just wear their colors. Some floats contradicted the ones before them, yet the crowd cheered for them all.

One float shouted:

STOP BEING LED—START LEADING.

Its voice roared like a football coach as screens flashed people climbing ladders, spotlights, and words like *grind* and *win.*

Then came the next—sleek, smooth, almost silent, draped in luxury and soft-purple tones. Its screens looped sun-drenched beaches, rooftop lounges, and flowing champagne. Across the top, in elegant script, it read:

STEP INTO THE EASY LIFE.

It didn't matter. The crowd cheered for all of it. Phones captured moments. Captions were posted mid-step. The parade kept flowing—new music, new slogans, new celebrity faces. Some walked with genuine excitement; others walked not to be left behind. Some shouted chants like prayers; others raised their phones like offerings.

The floats passed by like modern-day prophets, each declaring a new gospel: one promised purpose without pain, another offered identity without intimacy, a third proclaimed satisfaction without sacrifice. It looked and felt like worship, though no one would dare call it that.

A man stood mesmerized by the passing spectacle. The floats reminded him of unpursued dreams—quiet ones, carefully tucked away. Over time, urgency, deadlines, and a pressure he couldn't name had replaced them. Maybe the parade held something he hadn't realized he was searching for.

The music thumped—louder, harder to ignore. The floats passed by faster and faster. He tried to keep up, but everything blurred. The longer he watched, the more he felt himself fading. He wasn't sure what he was trying to find; he just knew he couldn't stop watching.

Then he saw her.

Between each blur of movement, on the opposite curb, stood a little girl—the only one not moving or watching the parade. She held a small handmade sign, just five words written in thick marker:

YOU HAVE NOTHING TO PROVE.

No one else noticed her. The crowds weaved around her without looking. To them, she was invisible, just another shadow on the sidewalk.

But he saw her—and she was looking directly at him.

He looked away, then back. She hadn't moved. Her eyes stayed fixed on him, her smile unshaken. Her unflinching directness—the way her gaze pinned him—unsettled him to his core. It was as if she were speaking directly to him without a word. Something about it made him deeply uncomfortable.

He rubbed the back of his neck. *"What does she want from me?"*

He turned toward the floats again. But their slogans felt louder now, more desperate.

He shifted his gaze back toward the girl—still there, still smiling, still holding that sign.

"What am I trying to prove?" he wondered aloud, then caught himself—startled to realize he'd spoken the thought aloud over the rumble of the parade.

For the first time, the thought cut through the clamor: had he been marching all this time to prove something—to measure up to a glittering image he could never hold together? The more he watched the floats drift by, the more he realized the parade wasn't carrying him forward at all; it fed that restless hunger to be seen, to be applauded, to be known.

He drew a deep breath. The weight on his shoulders lifted slightly; his chest felt looser, his breathing steadier. The music still pulsed, but it no longer held him as tightly as before.

He sat down on the curb and closed his eyes for a moment. The euphoric crowd surged around him without concern. The parade rolled on, but with his eyes shut, the music sounded out of tune.

He opened his eyes just as a gap appeared between two floats. The girl was still there, now holding a new sign:

YOU HAVE NOTHING TO HIDE.

His heart thumped. *"How does she know?"* The words slipped out before he realized he'd spoken. *"How could she... possibly... know?"*

The message pierced places he'd kept barricaded for years—the lies he'd rehearsed until they felt like truth, the polished persona he paraded in public, the fragile scaffolding that held up his carefully edited life. It scraped at the shame he thought he'd buried too deep to touch.

A flush of raw exposure swept over him—he couldn't bear to meet the eyes of the little girl across the street or face the sign she held, as if both had stripped him bare.

But she wasn't accusing him; she simply waited—smiling, assured, and still. Her focus unsettled him, yet somehow made him feel safe, as though she already knew everything and wasn't going anywhere.

He lowered his eyes to the ground. He hadn't realized how long he'd been pretending—pretending to have it all together, pretending to be important, pretending to be enough.

The floats rolled on behind him, shouting louder, brighter, faster, yet they felt smaller now—almost desperate.

Something within him was breaking. He didn't know what it was, but he knew it needed to happen.

He buried his face in his hands. For the first time in years, he didn't care who saw.

The music of the parade twisted into a painful cacophony—layers of noise pressing against him like a headache he couldn't escape. Covering his ears reduced it to a dull rumble.

When he looked up again, she was still there with yet another sign:

YOU HAVE NOTHING TO FEAR.

In that moment, his world collapsed—and then expanded.

The truth crashed over him like a breaking wave, stealing his breath. He saw how fear had threaded itself through every ambition, every late-night grind, every polished performance—fear of fading into the background, of being just another face in the crowd, of not being accepted, of never being worth loving at all.

But her words were not empty; they were a doorway. He didn't know exactly what came next, but he knew what had to end: the parade, the striving, the pretending, and the fear beneath it all.

He rose slowly and looked across the street, but this time she was gone.

Somehow, it made sense. He had received her message; *he had nothing to prove, nothing to hide, nothing to fear.* Perhaps someone already knew him, accepted him, loved him.

The little girl had been a messenger. Whoever she was, she had known the secret he was just beginning to learn.

He lingered for a moment, gazing at the spot where she had stood. Then, without looking back, he stepped away from the parade, moving against the tide of the ecstatic crowd. Behind him, its noise thinned into echoes, revealing what it had been all along:

Not a parade, but a distant, dissonant carnival.

THE LONG, DARK NIGHT

Depression, anxiety, and other emotional struggles are not signs of weakness or failure—they are real, often invisible burdens that can make even the simplest parts of life feel impossible. For many, the night can feel endless, and the darkness overwhelming. But even in those seasons when nothing seems to help and the light will not come; hope is not gone. Sometimes it arrives quietly. Not to fix us, but to sit with us. To remind us we are not alone.

... he even sees me in the dark! At night I'm immersed in the light! It's a fact: darkness isn't dark to you; night and day, darkness and light, they're all the same to you.

Psalm 139:11,12 (MSG)

It started like any other night. He turned off the light, pulled the blanket high, and waited for sleep to come.

It didn't.
Not after five minutes.
Not after fifteen.
Not after fifty.

He lay there as the night stretched itself thinner and thinner, like it might never end. The minutes slipped away, and time began to lose its meaning.

Something was wrong. He could feel it. The room was darker than usual.

He reached for the switch beside the bed and clicked it. Nothing. He clicked it again—still nothing.

With a strange urgency, he got up and moved to the wall. He flipped the overhead light switch. Nothing.

He stood in the dark for a long time, unsure if he was imagining it. Then, instinctively, he reached for his phone, tapping the screen to call up some light, a distraction, anything. But the screen stayed black. He tried again. Dead. Somehow, it hadn't charged—or perhaps it had, and the power had slipped away when he wasn't looking. Either way, it was useless now.

He tried the light in the hallway. Dead.
The bathroom. Dead.
The kitchen. Darkness.

He moved through the house as if it had turned against him. The silence was thick now—not empty, but full of noise. Thoughts louder than sound, fears louder than reason. He couldn't explain why, but something pressed against his ribs, as if his own breath had turned against him. Everything felt too loud and too quiet all at once.

He opened the front door, hoping fresh air might help. But even the street outside was dark. No moon, no stars, no city hum. Just a quiet that seemed to swallow everything.

He backed inside, closed the door, and leaned against it. He didn't know what to do. He had been here before—not this exact night, but he recognized this feeling. This darkness. It came sometimes, uninvited. Lingering longer than unwelcome dreams.

He tried what usually helped—slow breaths, counting backward, whispering prayers he hadn't said in years.

Nothing worked. Not tonight.

Eventually, he sank to the floor, legs folded beneath him. He wrapped his arms around his chest, as if holding himself together might stop everything else from falling apart. He didn't cry. Not really. But his eyes stung, and his throat tightened. He didn't know what he was afraid of—only that the fear was real.

He sat there for what could have been hours.

Then—a knock. So soft, he almost missed it. He froze. Another knock followed—slightly louder, but still far from insistent.

He rose slowly and felt his way toward the front door, one hand against the wall, the other reaching out in front of him. Every step he took was uncertain. His hand found the door frame and made its way to the doorknob.

When he opened it, more darkness met him. But in the middle of it stood a man, faintly illuminated by a small candle cupped in his hands. The glow of the flame danced across his face, soft and steady.

There was something about him. Not the way he looked, but the calm he carried—like someone who had already walked through this kind of night.

"*I thought you might need some company,*" the candle bearer said. His voice carried more warmth than volume.

The man blinked at the light. He still wasn't sure whether he was dreaming. "*Did you come to fix the power?*" he asked, voice rough from the long silence.

The other man shook his head. "No. *But I brought this.*"

He held out the candle. It wasn't much—certainly not enough to light a room. And yet it drew him in like warmth in winter.

He stepped aside to let the visitor in. The man entered without a word, walked to the center of the living room, and sat on the floor. He placed the candle between them.

The man sat down as well. Not because he knew what to say, but because of something about the flame that made the darkness seem... less final.

They didn't speak. The visitor asked no questions, offered no advice or solutions. He just sat there, as if he had all the time in the world. As if he knew silence—and didn't fear it.

The candle flickered. It didn't chase the shadows away, but it kept the shadows from winning. And that mattered.

He stared into the flame. Minutes passed. Then more. The night didn't end. The light didn't grow. But the space between his breaths widened.He wasn't better—but he wasn't alone. And that was new.

He looked up at the visitor's face glowing in the candlelight. "*Will morning come?*"

"Yes," the visitor said, his tone both soft and certain. "*But not yet.*"

He seemed to sense the man's unspoken thoughts. "*It's okay. I'll stay with you,*" the visitor said.

The light was still small. The darkness was still deep. But an indescribable peace surrounded them.

The man wished the lights would come back on. But for now, there was a candle—and someone to hold it with him.

And that was enough.

THE HIDDEN NOTES

Some voices wound. Others heal. And often, both speak in the same silence. It's easy to lean into the ones that echo shame—especially when they sound familiar, almost like our own. But we don't have to stay there. Another voice is speaking, too. It doesn't deny the damage. It simply dares the heart to hope again. The most life-changing messages rarely shout. They arrive quietly—unexpected, personal, and full of grace. The question is: which voice will you choose to believe?

With the arrival of Jesus, the Messiah, that fateful dilemma is resolved. Those who enter into Christ's being-here-for-us no longer have to live under a continuous, low-lying black cloud. A new power is in operation.

- Romans 8:1 (MSG)

She cleaned the early shift at the train station, arriving long before the crowds, before the announcements—before the day demanded more than she had left to give.

She used to work somewhere else—something with an office, a desk, and a nameplate she was proud of. But that ended quickly.

One mistake. A heavy one. Heavy enough for those above her to call it a disgrace—enough for her to believe them. So now she swept floors, cleaned toilets, and emptied trash cans. All she wanted was to keep her head down and try not to think too hard.

But she did think. Too much, if she was honest. She replayed moments, words, faces. She heard the old voices again in the quiet: the teacher who said she hadn't lived up to her potential, the boss who said she lacked initiative, the friend who slipped away after the fallout. Her own voice joined the chorus, *whispering regret in every silence.*

One morning, while sweeping the floor, she found a folded note left on the bench. Plain paper. Handwritten. Tucked just where she would find it. It read simply:

YOU ALWAYS RUIN EVERYTHING

The words hit hard—not because they were new. It was the kind of message she often whispered to herself. She didn't even question why it was there. Somehow, it felt inevitable.

The next day brought another, tucked beneath the base of a bench, half-crushed under someone's muddy heel. This one said:

EVERYONE KNOWS. THEY'RE JUST TOO POLITE TO SAY IT.

Her stomach dropped. It didn't accuse as loudly as the first, but it sank deeper. That fear had lived in her for years: the fear of being found out—of being seen and silently judged by people who smiled anyway. For the rest of the day, she avoided eye contact. Not because anyone looked at her differently—but because now she was sure they had been all along.

The next morning, she found a different kind of note. This one's handwriting was different—softer. Kinder:

THIS ISN'T THE END OF YOUR STORY.

It didn't accuse. It read like a whisper of hope she thought had died. She stared at it for a long time, then tucked it into her pocket—unsure why.

After that, the notes kept showing up. She noticed something peculiar: different colors distinguished the notes, not just their tones. The cruel ones were always on gray paper, the ink dark and heavy, as if scraped across the page. The gentle ones came in soft blues or sometimes even a deep violet that reminded her of dusk.

She didn't know why the colors mattered, but somehow they did. The blue notes let her pause, breathe, and even hope. The gray notes dragged her under—an undertow she couldn't fight.

Naturally, she sought out the blue notes. She'd even check the usual places twice, just in case she missed one. But when she found a gray note—no matter how hard she tried to ignore it—she unfolded it and read its contents.

She found some notes wedged behind vending machines, slipped under paper cups, and stuck between the cleaning cart's squeaky wheels.

Some were cruel—like fingers prodding an open wound.

EVERYONE KNOWS WHAT YOU DID.

NO ONE WOULD MISS YOU.

YOU'LL ALWAYS BE A FAILURE

Others were tender, and always unexpected:

YOU'RE NEVER TOO FAR GONE.

YOU ARE DEEPLY LOVED.

IT'S NOT TOO LATE TO BEGIN AGAIN.

The contrast made her pause and wonder. Were they from the same person or two different people? Or were they just figments and fragments in her mind trying to sort itself out? But the notes were real.

Someone had written them. And not just someone—*some ones.* Different hands. Different hearts. Different intentions. And yet, both had found their way to her.

These someones knew her. That was the part that haunted her more than the cruelty.

The kind words always felt undeserved—unearned, meant for anyone but her. She wasn't used to encouragement—especially the kind that didn't come with conditions, expectations, or strings attached.

Both kinds of notes landed deep. They echoed the argument she lived with every day. Her mind had become a courtroom, and these notes were the evidence—both for the case against her and for the one she hadn't dared to believe for years.

The cruel ones left her heavier, like cold, wet clothes she couldn't peel off. They named her failures and left her stuck in them. The honesty in the notes felt empty, like a description of the damage without showing how to heal it.

The others—clearer, quieter—never denied the damage. But they pointed beyond it, not with pressure, but with compassion.

They didn't say, *try harder.*
They said, I *see your tears.*

They didn't say, It's *hopeless.*
They said, I *am with you.*

Eventually, she gathered the notes. No matter what they said—kind or cruel—she collected them all. She wasn't sure why. Perhaps it was proof that someone had seen her. Maybe it was the need to make sense of the voices fighting for space in her head. But each one felt important, even the ones that wounded her.

She sat on the edge of the little table in the dimly lit custodial closet—the one where she ate her lunch in silence. She laid the notes out flat, paper soft from handling, some creased with sweat or tears. For a while, she just stared at them. Not reading—just remembering.

Each note—encouragement or accusation—had left a mark. And now, seeing them all together, she realized something she hadn't noticed before: the kind ones weren't just different in tone or color. They carried a quiet power the cruel ones lacked. A silent strength. Like a hand reaching out in the dark.

She wanted that strength to be true.

Even if she didn't feel worthy of it.

The next morning, she found a note that stopped her cold. It lay at the bottom of her cleaning cart—creased, dirty, and faded blue from months of trash bags she had emptied over it. She must have missed it all this time, hidden beneath the weight of the daily refuse.

Carefully, she unfolded it. These words were different. The words were neither comforting nor condemning, but a challenge:

YOU MUST CHOOSE WHICH VOICE TO BELIEVE.

She read the note repeatedly, her fingers tracing the words. The handwriting matched the softer ones. It wasn't accusatory—but it didn't back down either. It named the crossroad she had avoided. The war wasn't just around her. It was within.

The note was right—the decision was hers to make.

That night, one pile of notes went into the trash. The rest she folded—carefully, deliberately—and slipped into her bedside table. Not as a list of things to fix, but as quiet reminders of what remained true—even when she couldn't feel it.

In the days that followed, she moved more slowly through the station—and smiled more. There was a lightness to her step now, as if she carried something invisible but sacred. She listened closely, scanning the crowd—wondering if the writer was among them. She studied faces, postures, eyes—with quiet curiosity.

Now and then, she imagined stopping someone to ask: "*Was it you?*" But she never did.

It was enough just to be seen—and to walk as someone who knew she was worth seeing.

The station itself didn't change.
The shifts lasted long.
Still—something inside had changed.

Because she chose to listen to a different voice.
A voice that didn't deny her brokenness, but promised she'd never face it alone.

And a new story was unfolding—one she hadn't planned for, or even felt she deserved.

Yet someone offered it anyway.

THE SUBSTITUTE TEACHER

We often divide the world into categories—sacred and secular, spiritual and ordinary, meaningful and mundane. But what if those lines are blurrier than we think? What if the moments that matter most don't come from titles, positions, or platforms, but from quiet presence, unseen kindness, and the way someone makes a space feel different just by being in it?

Let every detail in your lives—words, actions, whatever—be done in the name of the Master, Jesus, thanking God the Father every step of the way.

- Colossians 3:17 (MSG)

She never taught in the same classroom for long—different day, different grade, different room. Sometimes math, sometimes music—sometimes just making sure no one set the library on fire.

She carried a canvas bag with sharpened pencils, hand sanitizer, peppermints, and a spiral notebook filled with margin-scribbles that made sense only to her. She wasn't impressive—at least, not by the district's standards. She never earned awards, never got her name on a plaque, and never once heard the words, "We'd love to make you full-time." But that never bothered her.

The students, though, noticed things—how she remembered their names after one day; how she smiled like she meant it; how she didn't flinch when the loud kid lost it; how she made even silence feel safe. Some kids sat taller when she was in the room. Others stayed quiet—but stopped looking over their shoulders.

She didn't carry a Bible or quote verses. She didn't bow her head before lunch. But she did something most people missed: she walked into each classroom as if it already mattered—as if something invisible had been waiting there.

She believed in things other teachers didn't discuss in break rooms—like how kindness can shift an entire room's temperature, how a well-timed question can be more potent than a lesson plan, and how even fluorescent-lit hallways can hum with something unexplainably... good.

The subject never mattered much to her. It was the students—and the quiet, persistent nudge she always followed, though she could never explain why.

Once, a sixth-grade girl started crying during a vocabulary quiz. The substitute knelt beside her, not with answers, just presence.

"*I don't know why,*" the girl whispered later, "*but I felt calmer when she walked over and told me she believed in me."*

The teachers assumed it was good classroom management. The principal figured she was simply one of those naturally likable types.

One day, after subbing for a restless middle school class, she stayed behind to straighten desks. She noticed that someone had carved a name deeply into one; the letters scratched angrily. She rubbed her thumb across it, as if trying to soften the message someone had left behind.

Then she saw it—barely there, above the carved name, just beneath the laminate. A faint word, only visible when the light hit just right:

Holy.

She blinked, then looked again.
It was gone—or maybe it wasn't.

She checked another desk.

Holy.

And another.

Holy.

Each one was barely visible, only when the light angled just so.

No one wrote the words with a pen or marker. No one etched or smudged them. It was as if the desks had been stamped long ago, waiting to be seen.

She kept going.

The bookshelf—**Holy.**

The windowsill—**Holy.**

Even the corner of the whiteboard—**Holy.**

It happened again and again. Always faint, always fleeting—like the whisper of a secret too deep to say aloud.

She told no one. But she started looking. Not just at desks, but at lunch trays, lockers, textbooks covered in graffiti, even pencils chewed raw.

She started seeing beauty everywhere. Not the polished kind, but the hidden kind, a beauty that breaks your heart a little—then leaves it softer than before.

She never called it *sacred.* But she walked as if it were.

And in doing so, she taught lessons no curriculum could contain. Not with a whiteboard or lectures, but with attention and compassion—the quiet conviction that the line between sacred and secular had never existed.

Years later, many students would still remember her name. They would fondly recall how they felt the day she was in their class, how the room warmed up when she walked in, and how the pressure lifted for a day—like maybe they mattered more than a grade they received.

She didn't change the system.
She didn't start a movement.
She didn't go viral.

Still, every time she entered a room, she carried a whisper of something—more.

Something immeasurably more.

Something—**holy**.

THE CRITIC IN THE CAST

We live in a world drowning in commentary, where criticism often masquerades as conviction. It's easy to believe that pointing out what's wrong is the same as making things right. But what if our obsession with fixing others blinds us to our own responsibilities? What if the real problem isn't their flaws, but our failure to focus on the role we are meant to play?

"If I want him to live until I come again, what's that to you? You—follow me."

- (Jesus) John 21:22 (MSG)

It was the biggest news in the little town had heard in years.

A theatre producer announced the staging of a play unlike anything the town had ever seen. He called it a *"collaborative masterpiece"*—a production stitched together by hundreds of voices, movements, light, and heartbeat.

There would be no auditions in the traditional sense. No résumés. headshots. No lineups. Just a single invitation:

Come and take your place.
There's a role just for you.

They came from everywhere—young and old, loud and quiet, polished and raw. Some came chasing dreams. Others were unsure why they had even responded to the call.

One man lingered near the back, uncertain. He wasn't a singer, an actor, or a dancer.

But the producer approached and touched his shoulder. "*You'll be in Act Three*," he said. "*It's a pivotal moment. At the far left of the stage, when the lights go out, raise this lantern.*"

The man took the lantern with both hands, almost reverently. It was simple—made of brass—but it felt weighty in his hands. *My part may be small*, he thought, *but it must matter—why else would the producer ask me directly?*"

When rehearsals began, the man watched from the shadows as the others brought their parts to life. The leads were bold, expressive, and sometimes... theatrical. A few deviated from the script, improvising lines or adding flair. The ensemble added choreography that had never been in the notes. Some even suggested costumes that glittered more than seemed appropriate.

The man frowned. *This wasn't what the producer intended.*

Something heavier settled in his chest. *The cast is treating this like a stage for themselves, not a story worth honoring.*

That seed of criticism, once small, grew louder each day.

He shifted his focus from the lantern to his mental notes. He roamed backstage, whispering concerns to anyone who would listen.

"Did you see how she exaggerated that line?"
"That duet—they still haven't memorized the music."
"That guy in the second act? He's trying to steal the spotlight."
"I doubt the producer approves of this lighting."

Each night after rehearsal, he rehearsed his own critique, in case the producer ever asked for his opinion. All the while, his lantern gathered dust.

As opening night neared, his agitation grew. He had hoped the producer would step in—take control. But the producer stayed relaxed. Always smiling, moving among the cast. Offering quiet encouragement. Never showing concern.

Opening night arrived, and the theater pulsed with anticipation. The audience filled the house. The curtain rose.

From the side of the stage, the man watched the story unfold. There were mistakes, yes—but also magic. The audience laughed, cried, and leaned in.

Still, he couldn't stop noticing the flaws: an awkward entrance, a missed note, an actor who, he was certain, smiled too brightly for a sorrowful scene

As Act Three began, he glanced at the lantern sitting by the stage entrance. *I still have time*, he thought.

He leaned in to whisper a comment to a nearby stagehand. "*This part always drags. They should have cut it. If I were in charge, I would—*"

Then it happened—the blackout.

His cue.

His eyes darted to the darkened stage, now cloaked in confusion. The actors stumbled, unsure where to go. Timing unraveled. Lines faltered.

He had missed his moment.

The man stood motionless—the unlit lantern still sitting beside him. Too late, he reached for it, but the scene had already passed. The moment moved on—so did the story.

By the final curtain, he was still standing in the wings—lantern untouched.

After the crowd had gone and the cast had trickled out, the producer found him sitting alone in the place where he was supposed to have raised the lantern. The man lowered his head.

"*I was only trying to protect the integrity of your work.*"

The producer didn't answer right away. He stepped toward the stage, surveying the empty house. Then, still facing the rows of vacant seats, he spoke softly but firmly.

"*I never asked you to direct. I asked you to play your part.*"

The man looked down at the lantern. It looked heavier now—not because it had changed, but because of what it might have meant.

The producer turned to face him.

"The moment went dark because the light I entrusted to you never left the shadows."

His words carried no anger. Only truth. And the truth was enough.

The producer placed a hand on the man's shoulder.

"It wasn't the missed notes or extra sparkle that broke the moment."

He let his hand fall, a quiet sigh escaping.

"It was the absence of the part I asked you to play."

The producer walked away—his footsteps the only sound in the empty theater—already preparing for the next performance.

THE MISSING CAMPER

It takes courage to leave the comfort of the crowd in search of someone who's gone missing—especially when that person has broken the rules, worn out their welcome, or made things difficult. But genuine love isn't calculated by fairness or efficiency. It risks discomfort, criticism, and even rejection to bring someone home. Because to love like that is to believe that one life—no matter how messy or misunderstood—is worth everything.

"Suppose one of you had a hundred sheep and lost one. Wouldn't you leave the ninety-nine in the wilderness and go after the lost one until you found it?"

- (Jesus) Luke 15:4 (MSG)

A group of young campers gathered around a crackling fire, its warmth cutting through the stillness of the forest beneath a ceiling of pine and stars.

The group wasn't large, but it moved like a single body—tents pitched with precision, meals eaten on time, fires lit and doused according to the leader's rules.

The leader had no badge or whistle, but when he spoke, even the trees seemed to listen.

Among them was one who never quite fit. A boy—lanky, loud, restless. He tied knots the wrong way, trampled boundaries marked with orange twine, and once tried to roast a marshmallow with a lighter he'd smuggled in his sock. He wasn't cruel, just always a little off from the rhythm of the others. Some rolled their eyes. Some muttered behind his back. A few simply wished he'd go away.

That night, after the fire was out and the stars had taken their places, the boy slipped into the woods.

The leader had warned them earlier—as he always did—with the same words they'd come to expect:

"Don't wander off alone. The woods can be dangerous after dark."

But the boy had never listened before. Why start now?

It was a sharp-eyed camper who first noticed the empty sleeping bag. At first, the others whispered. Perhaps the boy was nearby—just off to pee. Maybe he wandered just past the firelight to be annoying again. But when time stretched, and the boy did not return, the group stirred with unease.

The leader stood, counted faces in the dark, then stood still for a moment longer, staring into the trees.

"*Stay here,*" the leader said firmly. "*Do not leave the fire.*"

"*Wait—where are you going?*" one camper called out.

"*To find him.*"

"*But what about us?*" another camper asked, glancing into the dark woods.

"*You're safe. I'll be back.*"

"*But he broke the rules!*" someone blurted.

The leader didn't respond. He was already moving, flashlight in hand. His silhouette was swallowed by the branches. His footsteps faded into the hush of the forest.

The campers waited. The night grew colder. The fire dimmed. The woods pressed in with silence—broken only by the occasional snap of a twig or the rustle of wind. Some murmured with concern; others grumbled in frustration. A few stood silent, eyes fixed on the path where their leader had vanished—still wondering what made that one boy worth the risk.

Minutes passed. Then an hour. Restlessness turned to unease.

Just as worry began to take hold, two figures appeared at the edge of the trees. The boy walked with a limp, and dirt streaked across his cheek. The leader's shirt was torn, his hands scraped, and a darkening bruise marked his left forearm. But they were both smiling.

The group rose to meet them with a strange mix of relief and resentment. Some campers scoffed as the boy approached the fire. A few laughed under their breath. One mimicked the boy's limp behind his back.

"*Aww... look who finally wandered back. Couldn't hack it out there?*" one camper sneered.

A few other campers snickered.

"*Told you he'd come crawling back,*" another jeered, elbowing his friend. "*Hope it was worth it, loser.*"

Laughter broke out, loud and merciless.

The boy said nothing. He lowered his eyes and sat near the fire, shoulders drawn tight, as if he wasn't sure he still belonged.

The leader turned slowly to face the group. His voice was calm, yet carried weight.

"*Do you think he's different from you? Do you think wandering only happens with your feet?*"

He surveyed the group of young campers, making eye contact with each one.

"*Some of you have stumbled this entire trip—tripping over your pride, your fear, your judgment.*"

He smiled, yet his voice held more passion than warmth.

"*Don't you see? I would've come after any single one of you.*"

The leader crouched near the embers, warming his fingers without another word.

The boy sat beside him, quieter than anyone had ever seen him.

For a minute, no one spoke. They just sat around the fire in the stillness of the moment, breathing in the smoke and silence.

Then the boy looked over. There were scratches on the leader's hands, angry red lines from brambles and branches. His knuckles were raw with drying blood into the creases. A purple bruise bloomed beneath one eye, the skin swollen from a fall.

The boy said nothing. But his eyes lingered on the wounds longer than he meant to. He realized those marks weren't from the previous day's hike. They were from the leader's pursuit of him. Every wound carried the shape of a choice—a decision to leave comfort behind for someone who had wandered off.

The leader must have known the boy was staring. His eyes flicked to the boy, then moved from face to face around the circle before coming to rest on the glowing embers in front of them.

Still gazing into the orange coals, he whispered, "I *went after him... because he matters.*"

The others remained silent as the fire popped and crackled, and the wind rustled through the trees.

One by one, the young campers returned to their sleeping bags.

But the boy remained seated beside the leader, watching the flames. His mind replayed the most reassuring words he'd heard in a very long time:

"*...because he matters.*"

THE INVISIBLE FRIEND

Some children just know. Not in the way adults explain things. Not with logic or rules or reasons. Just a quiet awareness—like sunlight on skin—that someone is near. Invisible, but somehow real. It's not pretend. Not made up. It's what happens when a child's heart is still tender enough to sense the presence of someone beyond explanation. A presence that listens. That stays.

But then something breaks. Innocence gives way to upheaval. Wonder is replaced by survival. And that once-familiar nearness feels far away—or worse, like it was never there at all. Is there a way back? Can what once felt so real still be true?

If your heart is broken, you'll find God right there; if you're kicked in the gut, he'll help you catch your breath.

- Psalm 34:18 (MSG)

When she was young, she had an invisible friend.

Not the kind her classmates bragged about—the mischievous ones who tipped over juice cups or left the bathroom light on.

Hers was different. He didn't play tricks or demand attention. He simply was.

He was invisible, yes—but not imaginary. He was intimate. He never interrupted, never scolded, and he never left.

And he always listened.

She couldn't remember the first time he showed up. There was no pretend tea party, no grand introduction. It was more like she just started noticing she'd never really been alone.

As if he had always been there, close enough to hear her heart-beat.

Maybe it began with the picture-book stories and whispered prayers—the ones about a man who stilled storms, touched out-casts, and saw people no one else noticed.

She believed in the stories. She believed in *him*. Not because she understood, but because something deep inside her knew they were true.

When she talked to him, it felt as if he answered—never in words, yet somehow she heard him. She whispered to him in the hallway closet, where the shadows stretched like long fingers. His pres-ence made the dark less frightening. She talked to him on the backyard swing when the sky pressed down with its questions. Even when she said nothing at all, she sensed he was there—lis-tening.

He was there for scraped knees, birthday candles, lonely walks home, and secret joys.

Though no one else could see him, she never doubted he was real.

Until that night.

The night the door creaked open and something was taken that should never have been touched.

She didn't have words for it then—only the feeling that her body had been rewound and rewritten. Something inside her curled in on itself like burnt paper. And for the first time, she couldn't feel her invisible friend. Not because she looked and he wasn't there, but because she didn't look.

She couldn't. The places where he had once felt near were now too sharp, too quiet. She avoided them—avoided the stillness, avoided herself. Slowly, the warmth she had known faded into something she stopped trying to remember.

Maybe he was never real. Maybe I made him up—just a dream I clung to until daylight burned it away.

The silence didn't feel like absence.

It felt like erasure.

It stung like betrayal, and pain built walls so thick that even love felt distant. Beneath the questioning, something darker stirred.

She didn't say it aloud at first, but the questions throbbed beneath the quiet: *If you were really there... why didn't you stop it? Why didn't you protect me?*

She wanted to throw something. Or scream. Or forget. Instead, she folded the questions and hid them in the same corner where she had buried her belief.

It felt safer to feel nothing than to admit how much it hurt—how angry she was, how betrayed.

She stopped talking to her invisible friend altogether. Buried him in the vault where forgotten things go.

She tried not to feel. But sometimes the ache pressed in too hard, and she didn't know where to put it. So she found quiet ways to let it out—nothing anyone would notice.

Just a scratch here, a cut there. Enough to feel in control of something.

Years passed. Life layered itself over her like coats she couldn't take off—responsibilities, relationships, recognitions that never felt like enough. Her days became full of people, her nights full of noise.

And in the middle of it all, she ran. Not with her feet, but with her heart—chasing freedom like a runaway balloon.

She made bold choices. Loud ones. Some brave, some reckless. All of them were trying to prove something. She just wasn't sure what.

She never let herself cry. Crying would make it real. Crying meant it still hurt. So she pushed it down—buried it beneath achievements, perfect smiles, well-timed sarcasm. Over time, it became manageable. Heavy, but hidden.

Yet in the quiet afterward—after the nights that left her emptier—something deeper stirred. It was an ache. Not just for clarity, but for safety. Not just for answers, but for a presence. The steady sense that she was not alone in the dark.

She missed what she had once known so long ago—without

knowing how to find it again.

Then, on a rainy afternoon—after a week of heaviness she couldn't name—she wrapped herself in a blanket, curled into the corner of her couch, and let the silence ask the question for her: *Are you still there?*

She didn't expect an answer.

And yet, there it was. Not in words. Not even in thoughts. Just something she hadn't felt in a very long time: the warmth of being seen. The hush of being known. The weightless relief of being loved.

It was him.

Not dramatic. No flash of light, no booming voice—just a stillness that moved.

And somehow, she knew he remembered everything.

Every moment she had tried to forget.

Every tear she had never let fall.

There was no explanation—just presence. But in that presence was something stronger than answers: a grief larger than her own, a knowing that ran deeper than her rage.

She realized then—he hadn't looked away. He had felt it all.

And he had never left.

Not even when she did.
Not even when she blamed him for abandoning her.
Not even when she couldn't bear to love someone who hadn't stopped the worst.

Her childhood had been stolen, and she had wandered so far into grown-up expectations and fears that she had forgotten what it felt like to be still, to be small, to be held.

And he was still listening. Still near. Still intimate.

Since that day, she talks with him often. But now, it's deeper. More honest.

Still childlike, but not naïve.

Not always with words—sometimes with tears, or laughter, or silence. She tells him things no one else would understand—things that aren't problems to solve or prayers to be granted, just pieces of her she wants to share.

Not because she's searching for answers, but because he's still her best friend. Closer than thought. More vivid than imagination. Truer than anything she can explain.

And now she's beginning to see—he knows her better than she knows herself. Not the version she performs, but the one beneath the layers. The one marked by wounds she still can't name. The one she once believed no one could love.

And yet—he stays.

Not just with her, but for her—carrying the weight of what was taken, holding the pieces she thought were lost forever.

Now she knows he will never leave or abandon her.

That knowing gives her the courage to keep moving forward...

... never alone, and a little more whole each day.

THE BREAK ROOM CONVERSATIONS

It's easy to think gossip is harmless—just words tossed around in the *safe* corners of the day. But what's whispered in private rarely stays hidden. In time, even the quietest of conversations can rise to the surface, revealing more about us than the ones we speak of. When truths finally surface, what will our words say about us?

Watch the way you talk. Let nothing foul or dirty come out of your mouth. Say only what helps, each word a gift.

- Ephesians 4:29 (MSG)

It was just an ordinary break room—small, boxed in by glass walls, lit by harsh fluorescent lights.

It had no personality: a few tables, a counter with a sink, a microwave overdue for a scrub, and a small refrigerator humming in the corner.

Scuffed tiles and sticky spots marked spills that had never been mopped up. The air smelled of burnt popcorn, reheated pasta, and forgotten leftovers. In other words, it smelled exactly like a break room.

It was the place where ideas brewed with the coffee, complaints simmered like leftover soup, and conversations clattered louder than dishes in the sink. Over bowls of ramen and third cups of coffee, it became the workplace's unofficial hub—casual, convenient, and just private enough to feel safe.

If something needed to be said—but not said too loudly—it happened there. The break room didn't demand gossip, but it welcomed it. No one planned it that way. It just became that kind of room.

It started innocently enough: frustrated sighs, minor complaints, a bit of speculation between meetings. Then came the shared smirks—the jokes with just enough truth to sting. Judgments disguised as concern. Stories passed as fact. Jabs that sounded like jokes—until they didn't.

Truth was bent to make a story more intriguing. Silence signaled assumption. And reputations unraveled in the shadows. No one thought of themselves as a gossip. They were just...

"... being honest..."
"... letting off steam..."
"... saying what everyone already knew."

Everyone contributed to the chatter. And in time, everyone became its subject.

On a typical Monday morning, the office staff arrived to find the break room transformed. Dozens of white sheets papered the glass walls, each printed with plain black text—fragments and full conversations.

There were no names, but everyone knew.

It was a transcript. Every whispered comment. Every sarcastic remark. Every quiet accusation and assumption shared in that room over the past month.

And it didn't stop there. There were screenshots of texts, private messages, and group chats. Conversations once thought safe were on display for all to see—no names, just words. Somehow, that made it worse.

The words were louder now, echoing and exposing. Silence pooled in the room, broken only by the occasional sigh or drawn breath.

People gathered outside the glass to read. Some skimmed quickly. Others stood frozen. A few turned away, wide-eyed in shock. Some walked off and never returned for a second look.

Almost everyone recognized something—a phrase they'd spoken, or words spoken about them.

No one claimed responsibility. And that made it worse. There was no one to interrogate or confront. Just a wall of words and a reflection no one wanted to see.

Soon, the silence turned to whispering again—this time in tones of fear and blame.

"This went too far."
"It's an invasion of my privacy."
"Who's behind all of this?"

The discomfort of exposure searched for someone to blame, but found no one. There was only the truth. And the truth, stripped of its disguise, was harder to ignore.

That day, the office buzzed with theories. Was it a hacker? A prank? A sting operation from HR?

The next morning, a single note appeared on the bulletin board outside the room. Someone had handwritten it with a thick black Sharpie. No one recognized the hand that wrote it:

What we allow ourselves to say out loud—
reveals who we are on the inside.

The note didn't shout or scold, but somehow it spoke louder than anything else that week.

No one removed it. No one dared.

The break room changed after that. Not physically—the microwave still groaned, the refrigerator still smelled—but the atmosphere shifted. The clatter of coffee cups continued, but the smirks and whispers were gone.

The room lost its power—or maybe its permission.

People became quieter. Not out of fear, but out of recognition, respect, even reverence. They chose their words more carefully. They paused before responding. Some started asking before assuming. Others began listening before concluding.

Others apologized—with small gestures.

A coffee refill for someone once misunderstood. A shared table with someone who'd felt left out. A pat on the back long overdue.

Gradually, something sacred replaced the suspicion.

One afternoon, someone brought in homemade cookies. Another brought extra snacks. Someone finally cleaned the microwave and the refrigerator. Little by little, grace took the place where gossip once lived.

A few days later, a new handwritten note appeared on the bulletin board. Same marker. Same mystery.

The second note didn't explain itself. It didn't need to. It lingered likc a whisper no one wanted to lose:

Whatever we build on truth
and guard with trust—
becomes a treasure.

THE NAMETAGS

We spend much of our lives carrying names—not the ones given to us at birth, but the ones that found us later. We heard some names whispered in moments of failure. Others were shouted by rejection or silence. A few we survived, and others we accepted because we didn't know we had a choice. But what if the truest names aren't the ones we've inherited, earned, or endured—but the ones revealing how something greater, beyond us, sees us, knowing who we truly are?

Don't be afraid, I've redeemed you. I've called your name. You're mine.

-Isaiah 43:1 (MSG)

He carried a case—unremarkable at first glance. Its corners were frayed, edges softened by time. But when opened, the inside revealed rows and rows of nametags.

They weren't like the cheap, disposable kind you'd find at conferences. These were different. Solid. Each one was brushed steel, engraved with a single word—deep, unique, unchangeable. A name. Not a name given at birth, but one chosen long before they were conceived.

He never asked for introductions. He didn't need to. He would simply look at someone—really look—and then open the case, select a tag, and offer it without explanation.

To a woman who had spent most of her life afraid, speaking in apologies and standing near the edges of rooms, he gently fastened a tag over her heart.

It read: **Brave.**

She let out a quick, nervous laugh. "*You must be* mistaking *me for someone else.*"

"*I don't make mistakes,*" he said with a sincere smile and a quick wink.

Later, he noticed a man leaning against his car beneath the looming shadow of a glass-and-steel high-rise. The man's tie hung crooked around his neck, his eyes vacant. Moments earlier, security had placed a cardboard box in his arms and escorted him out—no eye contact, no explanation, just silence and protocol. Now he stood frozen, as if the world had moved on without him.

Without speaking, the man with the case walked up to him, stopped just short, and extended a small nametag between them.

The nametag displayed one word: **Trustworthy.**

The man didn't reach for it. Perplexed, he stared at the tag. "*That's not me. Not anymore,*" the man said, his voice frayed with regret.

The name giver smiled. "*I haven't forgotten who you are.*" He touched him on the shoulder and walked off.

To someone who had spent years giving herself away—piece by piece—in search of affection, acceptance, and survival, he held out the nametag that said, *Pure.*

She recoiled, her voice low and heavy with shame. "No... *you don't know the things I've done.*"

He looked at her—not with pity, but with honor. "*I've known you longer than you've known yourself.*"

He fastened the tag gently over her heart. She began to cry—not from shame, but because something broken was being restored.

The name giver moved on.

He gave a nametag that read:

Kindhearted to someone with anger in his eyes.

Loved to someone who had long given up on reconciling with her parents.

Whole to a man who had only ever known brokenness.

Free to one tangled in addiction.

At first, most resisted.

"*It's too much.*"

"*It's not true.*"

"*I can't accept this.*"

But he never argued. He just smiled and placed the tag where it belonged. Not on a sleeve or jacket, but always over the heart—as if that was the only place strong enough to carry something so permanent.

The metal felt warm. It couldn't be removed—not by shame or denial, not even by disbelief. Once placed, it stayed.

People walked away wearing names they didn't feel ready for. Some hid them under scarves or avoided mirrors. However, the new names stirred up something beyond explanation.

Days later, the woman named **Brave** stood up for someone else without realizing it.

The man named **Trustworthy** told the truth at the next job interview.

The one named **Kindhearted** softened and saw the brokenness in others.

And the woman named **Pure** began to carry herself as someone worth cherishing.

They didn't become their name overnight. But the moment they received it, they saw themselves in a different light for the first time—a clearer lens, a truer reflection.

Not everyone accepted their nametag. Some pulled them off before they could stick, dropped them in gutters, or buried them in junk drawers. But even then, the names had a way of resurfacing—at just the right moment; a glimpse in a reflection, a phrase from a friend, or simply a feeling that refused to be forgotten.

The man with the case never forced a tag on anyone. He never explained how he knew. But when asked, his answer was always the same: "*I restore what always was.*"

One day, a child tugged on his coat. "*Do you have a name too?*"

The name giver looked down and smiled. Then, kneeling slowly, he opened the inner flap of the case. There, resting alone, was a nametag unlike the others. Its edges were worn smooth by time and touch.

The engraving shimmered—not with heat, but with presence.

Whatever it said, the child couldn't read it. Not yet. But something about it felt familiar—like a name he'd always known but couldn't remember. Like a whisper that lived deep inside his chest.

The child smiled, without knowing why.

And as the name giver stood and continued on his way, those he had named stood a little taller, walked a little freer, and spoke a little truer. Not because they had earned a name, but because he had seen them—

...not for what they had become, but for who they were always designed to be.

THE MERCY LIGHT

Sometimes it feels like the world is growing colder. Acts of kindness that once seemed natural now feel rare, and help often comes with strings attached. But deep down, most of us still long for a place—or a person—where mercy flows freely, where no one has to prove their worth before being welcomed. What happens when that kind of light begins to fade?

"I was hungry and you fed me, I was thirsty and you gave me a drink, I was homeless and you gave me a room, I was shivering and you gave me clothes, I was sick and you stopped to visit, I was in prison and you came to me."

- (Jesus) Matthew 25:35 (MSG)

The lighthouse had stood for generations.

It was perched high on a cliff overlooking a rugged coastline. Its sweeping beam once sliced through fog, storms, and the darkest nights. They called it *The Mercy Light*. It was more than a landmark; it was a lifeline. When storms raged and ships lost their way, the lighthouse offered more than direction—it offered rescue. It offered hope.

The keepers of the tower were quiet souls. They never sought recognition or reward. Their strength came from tending the flame, watching the horizon, and rowing into danger before anyone else even realized trouble had come. Above the door of the tower, their creed was carved in wood:

SHINE THE LIGHT.
RESCUE THE LOST.
WELCOME THE BATTERED AND BEATEN.

They kept no records of how many they had saved. That wasn't the point. For a while, it seemed their work had paid off. The sea grew calmer. Fewer distress flares pierced the sky. Some believed the worst was behind them.

But time has a way of dulling memory. As silence settled over the water, comfort crept into the tower. Some welcomed the calm as proof they'd prevailed. Others, though, grew uneasy.

"*Are we forgetting what the light is for?*" one keeper asked softly. But his question fell like a feather onto a pillow.

Soon, a different concern emerged. *What if the danger comes from the land instead of the sea?*

The mission began to shift. First came the gate—"*just a precaution,*" they said. Then came the walls, first low, then higher. Locks were added. Guards were hired. Protocols were revised.

"*We must protect the light,*" declared a keeper at a meeting. His arms were crossed as he spoke. "*There are those who would misuse or abuse it.*"

Eventually, new keepers were appointed—not for their compassion, but for their compliance. The old creed above the door was replaced with a new one:

FOR THOSE WHO BELONG.

The light still shone, but not for everyone. Rescue became conditional. Those seeking help now had to meet specific criteria—shared beliefs, proven trustworthiness, alignment with the tower's values.

And when shipwrecks still happened—as they always do—the keepers held meetings instead of launching boats.

"*Where are they from?*" someone asked, eyes narrowing as if distance itself carried risk.

"*Do they believe what we believe?*" another pressed, tapping a finger against the table as if the answer would steady the storm inside.

"*Will they respect our way of life?*" a third questioned, the words more guarded than curious.

Discussion replaced action. Caution replaced compassion. The flame that once projected hope became more of a symbol—less mercy, more membership. The tower had never stood taller, yet its reach had never been shorter.

Still, the sea cried out.

In a dusty corner of the tower, beneath a broken lamp, an old journal lay forgotten. It wasn't an official log—just a weathered notebook filled with personal reflections from one of the early keepers. Its pages told stories of rescues in darkness, of impossible risks taken without hesitation, of joy overflowing when even a single life was pulled from the deep. Some pages bore witness to the ultimate cost—lives lost not in vain, but in the sacred act of trying to save another.

One night, a young apprentice discovered the journal. She read its stories in silence, her fingers pausing over a water-stained line:

Go, even when it's uncertain...

Love, even when it's costly...

Shine, especially when it's dark...

That same night, a storm rolled in—sudden and fierce. A fishing boat radioed for help, trapped between jagged rocks and pounding surf.

The keepers stood behind the glass, watching the waves batter the vessel.

"*We don't know who they are,*" one keeper admitted, voice catching on the unease. "*Or if they're like us.*"

No bell rang. No team was dispatched. No rescue boat was launched.

By dawn, the fishing boat had vanished. And though the light at the top of the tower still flickered in the distance, the question lingered in the salt-heavy air:

Who was it shining for now?

Weeks passed. The apprentice kept returning to the journal, reading the same lines until they felt etched into her hands. Each return to the worn pages left her staring longer at the sea, wondering if the stories still mattered. The wind against the tower windows felt like a summons she could no longer ignore.

One night, with the sea growing restless and the wind pressing against the tower, she could not stay any longer. She took a small oil lamp, unhooked the lifeboat, and shoved it into the water. Without looking back, she began to row alone into the dark.

She didn't know if anyone needed saving that night. That wasn't the point.

They say she never returned.

These days, some speak of a woman who lights her own fire somewhere down the coast and waits for storms the tower no longer sees.

But sometimes, on nights when the waves snarl and heave, those lost at sea speak of a smaller light—low and near, not from a lofty tower but from the water itself.

A light that doesn't ask questions...

... and comes for anyone in need of rescue.

THE PRISONER'S MOTHER

There's a kind of love that doesn't make headlines. It shows up quietly, without applause, and keeps showing up even when it's rejected, ignored, or misunderstood. It's unconditional—not based on behavior, reciprocation, or worthiness. It doesn't say, "I *love you, but...*" Because that isn't really love at all. True love doesn't ask, "Is this working?" It simply asks, "Is this right?" It holds on when others let go—not because it's easy or logical, but because something deeper compels it—a fierce, steady refusal to give up on someone, even when everyone else already has.

But God demonstrates his own love for us in this: While we were yet sinners, Christ died for us.

- Romans 5:8 (NIV)

Every Thursday morning, she came. Same gray coat. Same scuffed shoes. Same paper bag clutched in wrinkled hands. Her walk was slow but steady, like someone who had long ago decided that faithfulness was more important than speed.

She passed through the front gate of the prison without fanfare. The guards knew her by now. She never made small talk. Never asked for favors. She simply handed over the paper bag and signed her name on the visitor list—even though he never came.

Her son had been imprisoned for almost a decade.

He was just a teenager when he went in—angry, hardened, and cold. She could still remember the day of his sentencing—how he refused to look at her in the courtroom, jaw clenched, eyes hollow. In the early years, he would see her. He'd sit across the plexiglass with arms folded and a scowl on his face.

Eventually, the visits became letters.

Then silence.

Somewhere along the line, he chose not to see her anymore.

Still, she came—week after week.

She caught the 6:15 bus, sitting near the window with the bag on her lap. Sometimes it rained so hard that she would be soaked the moment she stepped off the bus. Other times, the summer heat baked the plastic seat beneath her. Once, the bus broke down two miles from the prison, and she walked the rest of the way without hesitation. No one ever noticed. No one celebrated her loyalty.

But she came anyway.

And every week, she brought three things: A slice of cold meatloaf wrapped in wax paper—his favorite when he was a boy, even when it was dry. A handwritten letter, sealed. And a photograph from home—usually an old one. A memory from before.

She didn't know if he ever looked at them. But she brought them anyway.

The letters were always different, yet always the same.

"*I saw your old football coach at the store,*" she wrote, her pen pressing a little harder on the paper.

"*Your sister says hello,*" another letter noted, as if trying to keep the family's voice alive between the lines.

"*The dog still curls up on your bed—still waiting for you,*" she wrote, letting the sentence trail with unspoken longing.

Sometimes she wrote prayers. Other times, poems or scribbled pieces of Bible verses. Once in a while, she just wrote what she wished she could say out loud:

"*I miss you,*" written softly, the ink trembling with memory.

"*I love you so much,*" another letter professed, like an ache she refused to silence.

"*I believe in you,*" she wrote again and again, as if willing the ink might seep through steel walls.

Every word said the same thing, really:

"*I will never give up on you.*"

It was the same as a promise carved in stone.

She remembered his laugh from when he was a boy—how he used

to chase lizards in the backyard, how he cried for days when his goldfish died, how he once made her breakfast for Mother's Day and filled the kitchen with smoke.

That little boy was still in there somewhere. She was sure of it. Because love never forgets.

But others had.

His crime had made the news. It wasn't petty theft or a youthful mistake. It was violent. Something people whispered about in grocery stores. Something that made neighbors cross the street.

Even in prison, his reputation set him apart. Other inmates kept their distance. He rarely spoke. He kept his head down. His silence was a wall.

And then there were **his mother's** few friends, some from her church, who urged her to let him go.

"*You did your best,*" one friend told her softly, as if pity could loosen her grip.

Others were less gentle. "*You don't owe him anything,*" another insisted, her tone clipped with finality.

Heads shook. Eyes narrowed. A few felt her pain and tried to make their persuasion sound like mercy.

"*Sometimes love means letting go,*" one woman offered gently, her tone firm despite the softness.

She never argued. She just kept showing up.

Some of the prison staff met her routine with veiled sarcasm.

"She's *a glutton for rejection*," an older guard scoffed under his breath, not caring who heard.

"*It's so sad. She needs to move on*," another whispered behind the reception room window, his eyes following her like a shadow.

A few saw it as noble. But most thought it was pointless.

The other prison visitors noticed her too. Some came once a month. Others only on holidays. They brought gifts, hugs, and tears—gestures wrapped in hope or guilt. Most came seeking something: a response, a change, a sign that it still mattered.

They called her "*the ghost mom*"—a name whispered by those who saw her every week, always silent, always alone, like a memory that refused to fade.

But she wasn't ageless. The years had marked her face, deepened the lines around her eyes. Loving her son had taken something from her—a cost she never spoke of, but wore plainly, like a garment she could never take off.

And that's why they pitied her—because they knew she would never stop coming.

But she didn't come every week for their sympathy. She showed up for her son.

One morning, a younger guard, who had watched her quietly for weeks, finally stepped forward. His voice was gentle but heavy with confusion.

"*Ma'am...*" The young guard hesitated, choosing his words as though stepping onto thin ice. "May I ask you something?"

She looked up from the sign-in sheet, her eyes both clear and tired.

"Yes?" she replied, her voice carrying both weariness and patience.

"Why do you keep coming? He won't see you. He tosses the food, the letters, the photos. He never answers... it's like he doesn't care that you come at all."

He'd meant the words to land gently, but the flicker of hurt that crossed her face told him they'd struck like a blow instead.

She held the bag for a moment, then handed it over as always. Her reply carried the quiet strength of someone who had made peace with pain long ago.

"Because he's my son," she said, her voice anchored in conviction, *"and nothing will ever change that."*

She turned toward the door that would take her back to the prison bus stop. But something made her pause. She looked back at the guard, her eyes welling, the shine of tears gathering, ready to spill.

She smiled—faintly but sincerely.

"I don't come because he opens the door," she added, a single tear tracing her cheek. *"I come because my love will never stop knocking."*

THE RIVER WALL

We all build walls—personally, corporately, even culturally. Sometimes to keep danger or pain out. Other times to protect the image we've worked so hard to present. But over time, cracks begin to form—hairline fractures from disappointments we didn't expect, failures we couldn't forget, and fears we've never fully faced. So we cover them up. We patch them with accomplishments, polish them with appearances, and add just enough beauty to convince ourselves—and everyone else—that everything is fine. But the cracks don't disappear. They widen. And deep down, we wonder: what if someone sees through it?

I'll give you a new heart, put a new spirit in you. I'll remove the stone heart from your body and replace it with a heart that's God-willed, not self-willed.

- Ezekiel 36:26 (MSG)

The city rose along the edge of a wide and well-traveled river. It was a beautiful place—green and vibrant—but the river had always been both a gift and a threat. It nourished the fields and carried trade, but it also had a history of rising in anger, swallowing streets, homes, and memories with a fury that left entire generations rebuilding from ruin.

After one particularly merciless flood, the people vowed—never again.

They built a wall—high, thick, and strong.

At first it was purely functional: a shield, a boundary, a way to sleep through the rainy season without fear. But time passed, and fear faded. The wall became something else—first a canvas, then a monument, finally a point of civic pride.

The city commissioned artists to cover its surface with sweeping murals: bright scenes of hope, heritage, and unity. With every new generation, the colors changed and the stories shifted, but the practice continued.

The wall was no longer just a defense; it became the city's identity.

No one spoke of the cracks that had appeared over the years. But they were there. At first, they were hair-thin, hardly visible. Later, deeper fractures formed—wide enough to collect rainwater, thin enough to whistle when the wind passed over them.

Some who lived along the wall noticed: a damp corner in the cellar, a patch of plaster that stayed cool after a storm, a subtle sag behind a framed photograph. But no one said much—not in public. After all, the wall looked beautiful. And beauty meant everything was all right, didn't it?

It was easier to paint. Paint was faster than repair, cheaper than truth, and more acceptable than asking questions.

The murals grew brighter, more intricate, more impressive—while the wall beneath them quietly grew weaker.

One early spring, before the season's first rain, a stranger arrived in the city. He was quiet, clearly from somewhere else. He carried only a worn satchel slung over one shoulder, filled with tools no one recognized. He didn't visit the galleries or wander the seasonal markets.

Instead, he walked the wall—Every day, one hand resting on the stone as though listening to it breathe, his eyes searching not for color but for what lay beneath.

"He's *listening to the wall!*" one of them whispered, barely able to hide a grin. The others stifled their laughter behind cupped hands.

"*Let him wander,*" a passerby muttered with a dismissive shrug. "*He'll be gone once the novelty wears off.*"

But he didn't.

He began to work—quietly, in small sections. Not painting, but rebuilding. From his satchel he drew stone and mortar, brushes of bristle and wire. He worked beneath the murals, removing sections where the fractures ran deepest and reinforcing what could not be seen.

Some grew angry.

"*He's defacing our history,*" one man barked, his voice edged with indignation.

Others shook their heads. "*What's he even trying to fix?*"

But one woman—a young mother whose home backed up to the oldest stretch of the wall—had been watching. For months water had crept through her foundation, staining her kitchen and stealing her sleep. She had patched, repainted, even prayed. Nothing held.

One morning she gathered her courage and followed the stranger. He was kneeling near the edge of town, fingers tracing a fracture that shimmered faintly in the morning light.

She edged closer from behind, then stopped, her gaze drifting over his shoulder. Her words trembled out: "*Could you... look at mine?*"

He stood, nodded with a small smile, and followed her home.

Inside, she lingered near the doorway, afraid of what might come next.

"*Can you fix it?*" she asked finally.

He knelt to examine the wall from within. It was worse than she feared—soft stone, deep decay, an illusion of strength that could crumble at any moment. He looked at her—not with pity, but with patience.

"I can," he said with gentle confidence. "*But to fix it, you'll have to let me rebuild it from the inside out.*"

His words unsettled her. "*But if you do that... everyone will see how broken it really is,*" she protested, her voice tight with shame.

He met her eyes, carrying both understanding and sorrow. "*Everyone is broken,*" he replied, meeting her gaze. "*Even if they pretend they're not."*

She didn't know if he was talking about the wall, about her, or about something else entirely. Still, she stepped aside and let him begin.

The first thing he did was strip away the paint. Generations of beauty peeled like skin, revealing the stone beneath—scarred and stained. Her neighbors gasped when they heard.

"You're ruining everything!" a neighbor shouted, her voice rising with alarm.

But she said nothing. She let the stranger continue his work.

He worked deep—not merely smoothing the cracks but rebuilding them from the inside out. He filled the fractures with something strange: a luminous material that caught the sunlight and shimmered even in the shadows, glowing softly in the rain.

He did not hide the repaired cracks. He didn't paint over them. A new kind of beauty emerged—unexplainable, living in what had once been broken but was now restored and whole.

When the next storm came, her home stood firm.

Others did not. The murals on their walls bled down the streets like ruined watercolor in the floodwater. The wall's gaping fractures opened wide, exposing the darkness that had been hidden within.

Gradually, others came—some with shame, others with questions, a few with tears.

"Is it too late?" one of them asked, almost whispering as if afraid of the answer.

He looked at them with a tender, reassuring smile that carried more comfort than words could.

"It's only too late if you never ask."

He welcomed them all kindly, without rushing or forcing.

Not everyone came. Some kept painting over the fractures and failures of their walls.

But those who let him work began to live differently. They no longer told stories of their strength—they told stories of surrender. They didn't boast of perfection—they spoke of the visitor who had rebuilt them from within.

And the wall?

It no longer looked pristine, but it shone with a beauty no artist could replicate. The cracks remained like healed scars—yet they were no longer shameful.

They had become sacred.

And the visitor—whose name few ever thought to ask—became known. Not for what he covered up...

... but for what he restored.

THE STREETLIGHT REVOLUTION

The world is more advanced and more connected than ever. But it's somehow darker, too. We look for someone to fix it—a leader, a law, a movement. We wait for the right person to rise, the right side to win, the right system to save us. But the change we long for doesn't come through power or platforms. It doesn't shout. It doesn't force. It starts in unexpected places—in quiet hearts willing to be the change rather than demanding it.

Don't put your life in the hands of experts who know nothing of life, of salvation life. Mere humans don't have what it takes; when they die, their projects die with them.

- Psalm 146:3,4 (MSG)

The city streets went dark.

Not all at once, but slowly—the kind of slow that sneaks up on you. A flicker here. A surge there. Until one night, no one could remember the last time the streets had truly glowed.

Some people blamed the leaders, some leaders blamed the people, but everyone blamed someone.

What used to be a city full of light—with open shops and music spilling from cafés, with children racing on bicycles past curfews, with couples walking hand-in-hand under amber halos of street-lamps—had grown quiet. Guarded. Closed. Dangerous.

Shops locked their doors before dusk. Parents pulled their children in early. People stopped making eye contact after dark. No one walked alone anymore.

But anger, like a spark, has a way of finding dry kindling—small at first, then suddenly a blaze that consumes everything near it.

One morning, a man stood in the center of the square, shouting as he held up a cardboard sign. The words were simple but demanding:

WE DESERVE LIGHT!

By evening, the square was crowded with angry voices, more signs, more slogans.

"*We've lived in the shadows long enough!*" a man shouted, his voice breaking as he thrust his sign higher.

Another protester jabbed their sign toward the mayor's office. "*It's time to demand what they've denied us!*"

"*No more fear!*" voices roared in unison.

"No *more hiding!*" others echoed, fierce and determined.

The chants overlapped—rising like a storm.

"*We'll organize!*"
"*We'll march!*"
"*We won't stop until we get what we want!*"

The people cheered at every promise that the darkness would end. They nodded at every bold speech about progress. They believed the leaders would bow to their demands.

Flyers appeared overnight. Websites launched. Committees formed. Videos flooded social feeds. And just like that, the *Streetlight Revolution* was born.

Week by week, the movement grew—rallies, protests, petitions. Candidates lined up promising light. Debates streamed in homes and cafés. The city buzzed with expectation.

But the streetlights stayed dark.

Crews came to replace the bulbs—they flickered once, maybe twice, then died again. Technicians blamed wiring. Politicians blamed each other. Experts formed panels and published reports.

Still, the streets remained dark, and frustration grew even louder.

Yet, near the square, on a quiet, cracked side street, someone did something different.

They brought out an old lantern—dusty, dented, almost forgotten. Cleaned the glass. Trimmed the wick. Struck a match. Then set it glowing on the porch.

There was no announcement, no speech, and no hashtag.

Just a simple light.

At first, the neighbors rolled their eyes. One called it *"nostalgic."* Another, *"naïve."* But something in its soft warmth made people pause.

On the third night, a woman across the street dug out a candle from the back of her kitchen drawer. A man down the block remembered a string of holiday lights in his garage. Someone else rigged an old reading lamp to a battery pack.

And the street began to glow again, house by house—not overhead, but eye-level; not from officials, but from neighbors.

People sat on their stoops again, watching as children played late into the evening and laughter drifted into the night air. Someone turned up a little music; someone else passed around cookies; another simply listened. The block was coming back to life.

Meanwhile, in the square, the revolution roared on.

A new voice rose—bold, charismatic, unyielding.

"New leaders, new future—that is what we demand!" she declared, her tone sharp as a bell. *"We must tear down the system to rebuild it. Demand our future!"*

She swept her hand toward the crowd. *"We will not rest until every light is restored!"*

"New leaders, new future!" became the chant of the day, echoing off stone buildings long after the rally ended.

But as the movement grew, it began to fray.

The angry mob needed the darkness to survive. Without unlit streets to rally against, the chants would lose their fire, the petitions their urgency, and the leaders their platforms. Solving the problem would have meant dissolving the cause itself.

Though no one admitted it, the revolution found purpose not in resolution but in perpetual unrest.

Eventually, the Streetlight Revolution collapsed. Factions formed. Leaders turned on each other. Some claimed it hadn't gone far enough. The bold-voiced woman stopped showing up.

Yet, far from the noise, something remarkable was happening.

Block by block, corner by corner, the glow kept spreading.

Lanterns appeared in windows. Twinkle lights wrapped around balconies. Cafés stayed open later. People gathered again—not to argue, but to be together.

Instead of speeches, campaigns, or a central plan, neighbors made light where they could.

And slowly—without a vote, without permission, without fanfare—the city changed.

One evening, a few weeks later, a woman wandered back to the square—quieter now, perhaps a little tired. She stood beneath a rusted streetlamp, staring up at the bulb that had never lit.

"Why didn't the revolution work?" she asked into the empty air.

A voice came from a nearby bench. "Because real change doesn't come by force or demand."

Startled, she turned.

There sat a man with a lantern in his lap—old, dented, still glowing. Something in its gentle light drew her closer, as though the glow itself refused to let her walk away.

She sat down beside him.

"*It begins,*" he said, his gaze steady on hers, "*when we take responsibility for our own hearts.*"

The two sat in silence as the lantern flickered between them—small but bright, casting enough light for the next step forward.

THE BUILDER

We all want to build something that lasts—something strong, admired, even remembered. But in a world obsessed with appearances, it's easy to forget that the most important parts of a structure are the ones no one sees. What if the real danger isn't in what we're building, but what we're building on?

A builder is more valuable than a building any day. Every house has a builder, but the Builder behind them all is God.

- Hebrews 3:4 (MSG)

He had spent years perfecting his life.

He shaped it with degrees, promotions, curated friendships, coordinated vacations. Even his furniture—everything spoke of precision and intention.

He didn't call it ambition; he called it progress. Every space in his life was carefully curated. Even his flaws were polished—to appear charming, self-aware, or at least manageable.

People said he was going places, and he believed them. But he never asked where.

At night, after the last emails were answered and the house had gone quiet, he would lie in bed and stare at the ceiling, wondering what the point of it all really was.

It wasn't sadness exactly; it was more like a quiet hum—low, constant, unrelenting. A restlessness he couldn't name. A question he couldn't silence: *Is this it?*

He tried everything—books, podcasts, therapy, meditation. He pursued romance, took exotic vacations, upgraded his wardrobe and his appliances. He filled his days with meaningful causes and occupied his evenings with mindless distractions. But the hum stayed, always there, just beneath the surface.

Sometimes it felt like he was walking through a beautifully staged home that wasn't his, the lights on, the furniture perfect, but no one truly living in it.

One early Saturday morning, desperate for fresh air or maybe just escape, he got into his car with no destination in mind. He drove without music, without a plan—just motion—hoping the movement might settle the ache inside. He passed suburb after suburb, then a golf course, a few warehouses, and a run-down strip mall.

Just as he came to the edge of the city, something made him slow down: a demolition site.

It was a building—maybe once a home—that was half-collapsed.

Wooden beams jutted out like broken ribs. Dust floated in the air like a morning fog. Bricks crumbled beneath rusted nails.

The entire scene looked as if it had exhaled its last breath.

Amidst the wreckage stood a solitary man with a sledgehammer, swinging with rhythm and purpose.

He slowed the car to a stop. He didn't know why—only that something about the scene pulled him in. He parked, got out, and walked closer, stopping just outside the temporary fence.

Shielding his eyes from the sun, he called out, "What is this place?"

The man lowered the sledgehammer, wiped his forehead with the back of his hand, and gave a half-smile. "My home..." He glanced around at the rubble. "...well, at least it was."

The visitor's eyes widened.

"You're tearing down your own house?"

"Yeah." The builder gave a tired chuckle. "It was beautiful once... people really admired it." He nudged a broken brick with his foot before going on. "But it was hollow. I built it to impress others, not to live in."

The visitor studied the splintered remains. "And now?"

The builder leaned on the sledgehammer. "Now I'm starting over. But not in the same way. No more rooms designed for performance. No more mirrors made to flatter. I want something real. Something honest... something human."

The visitor gave a dry, almost self-conscious laugh. "Sounds like a crazy dream to me."

"Maybe." The builder shrugged. "But some crazy dreams are truer than the lives we settle for."

Silence stretched between them. Then, almost without thinking, the visitor spoke, his voice quieter now.

"I've built something too. Maybe not literally... but it's there. Everyone thinks I'm happy. Sometimes I even convince myself I am. But deep down..."

He paused, swallowing hard.

"...deep down, it's like I've constructed something that isn't me."

The builder gave a slow nod, knowing well the man's dilemma.

"I chose everything for that house," the visitor continued, the words coming slower. "The paint. The floors. The view. But the foundation? I never really asked what it was sitting on. I think I just assumed it would hold."

After a beat, he gestured toward the rubble. "How did you know when it was time to tear it down?"

The builder's voice softened. "I didn't. I just knew I couldn't keep *pretending. Then one day...*" He took a deep breath. "*...I heard a voice.*"

The visitor looked at him, heavy with doubt.

"*What kind of voice?*" he asked, masking the creeping suspicion that the builder might actually be crazy.

A knowing smile tugged at the builder's lips. "*Someone who knows how to build what lasts. It was quiet, but clear—'It's never too late for a do-over.'*"

Another silence fell—just long enough to feel sacred.

The visitor looked down at his hands. They were strong, skilled, but tired. He thought of all the years spent stacking achievements, decorating his reputation, maintaining appearances. He thought of all the rooms full of things but empty of meaning.

When he looked up, the builder was holding out the sledgehammer. It was a gesture that was neither demanding nor dramatic—just open. His words echoed again in the quiet:

"*It's never too late for a do-over.*"

The visitor was at a loss for words, wondering if he might be crazy too. But a smile spread across his face. His fingers slowly closed around the handle.

THE TATTERED ROBE

Sometimes we give away parts of ourselves not because we want to, but because we don't believe we have a choice. The need to feel seen, accepted, or loved can quietly persuade us to trade our innocence—thread by thread—until we've lost what once made us whole. It's not always dramatic. It often happens slowly, in silence, and hoping someone will give back what others have taken. But deep down, many of us are still holding on to what's left, wondering if it can ever be restored.

He heals the heartbroken and bandages their wounds.

- Psalm 147:3 (MSG)

She never took it off.

She didn't remove it when she dressed for school. Not when she stepped onto the bus. Not when she walked into her first apartment.

You couldn't see the robe. It was invisible to everyone but her. Yet she could feel it—soft against her skin, woven from the love that didn't need to be earned. A quiet confidence. A covering of worth. She didn't know exactly where it came from, only that it fit and made her feel whole.

Until the day she started trading it away.

Just a little at first. The guy from English class said she had *"mystery in her eyes"* and invited her over. He didn't want to know her—he only wanted to be near whatever it was she carried. She gave him a thread, hoping he liked her as much as she liked him.

He didn't.

Then came the man who said she made him feel *"seen."* He didn't want commitment—just connection, just someone to listen, to care, to keep him from feeling alone. She gave him a piece too, hoping maybe... eventually... he'd want more than borrowed intimacy.

He didn't.

It didn't stop there. A professor who saw *"potential."* A boyfriend who needed *"to feel close."* A boss who promoted her, then used her. Each time, she gave something—a version of herself—hoping it would be enough to keep from being alone.

But the robe thinned.

She noticed it most when she was by herself, lying awake with unanswered texts or scrolling through carefully filtered photos of people who looked more complete than she felt. By her late twenties, the fabric hung off her like a question with no answer.

She tried to stitch it together with performance and positivity, with curated captions and filtered smiles, but the robe never hung quite the same. She didn't want only to feel loved—she wanted to feel whole again. But by now, she couldn't remember what that felt like.

Eventually, dating became a distraction. She said yes when everything inside her whispered no. She stayed in relationships that unraveled her further, all the while pretending she still believed in love. Sometimes, she'd stare at herself in the mirror and try to find the girl who used to feel safe in her own skin.

One morning, she sat on the edge of a bed that wasn't hers, staring at the sunrise through cheap blinds. She pulled her robe tighter, but it wasn't the cold that made her shiver.

She didn't cry. She just...sat. Numb.

The man beside her was still asleep. She slipped out quietly, put her heels on in the hallway, and walked the early-morning streets in silence.

That's when she saw him.

He sat on a bench that served as a bus stop, sipping from a paper coffee cup, smiling as if he had nowhere else to be. He didn't speak right away—just looked up as she walked by.

"*I know you.*"

His voice was soft, gentle, and sure.

She froze. She glanced around, as if checking for someone else.

"Excuse me?"

He nodded, still smiling.

"You used to talk to me."

She didn't recognize his face, but his voice sounded familiar. She knew she should feel uneasy around a stranger on the street, yet she felt comfortable. His voice reminded her of someone from her childhood. It felt...safe. She hadn't experienced that feeling in years.

He set the coffee beside him and motioned to the empty space on the bench. She sat—not because of his invitation, but because she was so tired.

They watched the city wake. Delivery trucks rumbled past. Dog walkers tugged at leashes. Third-shift nurses headed home in their scrubs. The air smelled of stale rain and warm bagels.

His eyes dropped, just briefly, to the torn fabric of the invisible robe draped around her shoulders.

"You... you can see it?" Her voice cracked with disbelief.

He nodded, a compassionate smile softening his expression.

She blinked back a rush of emotion. Her words came barely above a breath.

"No one else ever did."

"I always have." His reply was gentle.

She looked down at the robe—it was threadbare, uneven, and clumsily patched with borrowed scraps. She should have felt embarrassed, exposed, even humiliated.

But with him, she didn't.

"*I don't even know who I am anymore.*" The words slipped out before she could stop them.

He didn't respond right away. He just reached out—not to take the robe, but to touch the worn threads.

She flinched. It was instinct. Reflex. A lifetime of people taking more than they gave.

But he didn't pull back. He simply waited.

When she didn't move away, his fingers touched the fabric—the worn threads that told stories she didn't want to repeat. The missing fibers... the ones she believed disqualified her.

She wiped her cheek.

"*It used to be beautiful.*"

"*It still is.*" His voice carried a tenderness she hadn't heard in years. It made her feel safe... safe enough to be honest.

"*I used to be...*" She pressed her lips together, swallowing tears.

"*Beautiful.*" He finished her thought. Then he added, "*You still are.*"

She wanted to believe him. But the robe said otherwise.

"*It's ruined.*" She tugged at the fringe. "*I gave too much away.*"

He reached out again—not to take, but to touch the threads. The ones that held her pain and her past.

"*I can restore this,*" he said, examining the frayed edges. "*But only if you want me to.*"

"*Won't it always look... damaged?*"

"No." His voice held quiet conviction. "*It will look redeemed—and more beautiful than ever before.*"

She didn't know what to say.

For the first time in years, she felt the faint pull of something being mended—not by her hands, but by his. She looked at him—at his eyes that saw everything, at his hands that cradled her ruin like treasure.

Slowly, hesitantly, she loosened her grip on the robe. She wiped yet another tear from her cheek.

"*If you want to.*" She held out the edge of her robe with both hands, like a child offering something precious.

He smiled—the kind of smile that invited her toward a long-overdue rest.

"*I've been wanting to for a long time.*"

THE MAN WITH THE BULLHORN

We've all seen passionate people try to win arguments by raising their voices or shutting others down. But yelling doesn't change minds. What makes a difference is staying calm, listening carefully, and responding with respect. Real influence isn't about overpowering someone—it's about patience, clarity, and leaving space for change to happen naturally.

God's servant must not be argumentative, but a gentle listener and a teacher who keeps cool, working firmly but patiently with those who refuse to obey. You never know how or when God might sober them up with a change of heart and a turning to the truth.

2 Timothy 2:24-25 (MSG)

The man who shouted at people on the downtown corner had become a fixture. Every morning he arrived just after the sun rose high enough to light the steel-and-glass skyline. He wore the same scuffed boots, the same patched jacket, and the same hardened look. His stool squeaked as he unfolded it. He smoothed his sign as though it were sacred before propping it beside him. It read: REPENT OR BURN.

Gripping his weather-worn Bible in one hand and a bullhorn in the other, he began to preach. His voice cut through traffic and tangled with sirens, exhaust fans, and the pulse of street music. But unlike the city's rhythm, his cadence was sharp—urgent, harsh, unapologetic. He didn't smile. He didn't soften. He called it "*truth in love.*"

Few could see or hear the love in it. "*You in the short skirt! Have you no shame?*" he shouted. "*You with the long hair! God made you a man, not a woman. You in the rainbow shirt! Pride cometh before the fall!*"

Some yelled back. Others filmed him for entertainment. Many crossed the street early just to avoid him. Most just kept walking. To the preacher, their silence was proof of guilt—and of his effectiveness. Their discomfort was confirmation he was doing God's work. The angrier they were, the more righteous he felt. He saw himself as a prophet, misunderstood, maybe even hated—and for him, that made it holy.

Yet what he couldn't see was the slow hardening of his own heart. What started as fire had become fury. What began with tears now operated on outrage.

On a gray morning, as clouds pressed low and people hurried past with collars upturned, a man approached. He was average in appearance—nothing about him demanded attention. He didn't yell.

He didn't scowl. He simply stood there—calm, with a quietness that seemed to hush the street around him.

The preacher spotted him and flared instinctively. "*You here to laugh? To argue? To twist my words for some video?*"

The man shook his head slowly, palms open as if he had nothing to hide. "No. *I'm here to listen. To understand. Maybe even to help, if you'll let me.*"

The preacher's eyes flicked away. "Look... *I've been out here too long to think anyone stops just to listen.*" His voice thinned, barely reaching the bullhorn. "*They mock, they argue, or they turn their backs on God.*" He swept the crowd with his gaze, then leaned into the bullhorn, jabbing a finger skyward. "*Mark my words—they'll burn for it.*"

The man didn't react. His eyes remained steady, the silence stretching just long enough to suggest he was about to speak. "*May I ask you something?*"

Startled by the mild tone, the preacher lowered his bullhorn. "Go ahead," he said. *I'm ready.*"

"*When was Jesus angry?*" the man asked, his voice quiet and direct.

The preacher blinked, confused by the unexpected question. "What *are you getting at?*"

The man repeated, "*When did Jesus raise his voice in anger?*"

The preacher hesitated, as though pondering whether it was a trick question. "He *flipped tables in the temple. Drove out the heathen moneychangers with righteous anger.*"

"Yes," the man agreed, tilting his head slightly. "But *who was he angry with?"*

The preacher's brow furrowed, as if ready to seize control of the conversation. *"Those who turned God's house into profit—the religious leaders."*

The man's eyes didn't accuse—they grieved. *"And who wasn't Jesus angry with?"*

Frantically, the preacher flipped through his Bible as if to mount a defense, but the man laid a gentle hand over the open pages, steadying him.

"Jesus wasn't angry with the woman caught in adultery. He didn't scream at the man possessed by demons. He didn't shout at the thief on the cross. He didn't even attack the ones who drove nails into His hands."

He stepped closer and placed a hand on the preacher's sign. *"The only time Jesus raised his voice was when religion itself was used to block people from seeing God."*

The preacher looked at his sign and let out a breath he didn't know he'd been holding.

The man's voice softened. *"I'm not saying that talking about sin doesn't matter. I'm saying truth without love isn't holiness—it's just a hammer."*

He glanced around the intersection where pedestrians had slowed, curious, then looked back at the preacher. *"You don't have to yell for God to be heard. And you don't have to scare people into the Kingdom—Jesus never did."*

The preacher stayed silent, his rehearsed retorts stuck in his throat.

The man didn't linger. No mic drop. No dramatic exit. He patted the preacher's shoulder, then quietly turned away. He walked off into the crowd as if he belonged to it.

The preacher stood motionless. The street noise returned to its usual rhythm—horns, footsteps, voices. But inside, something had gone quiet.

He looked down at his sign.

For the first time in years, the words looked less like fire...

... and more like smoke.

THE GLOWING WINDOW

One can build a life like a house—full of rooms for work, rest, and joy. But over time, other rooms take shape too. Some stay locked. Other rooms develop different uses than originally planned. In quiet corners, certain habits or escapes begin to feel safe, even comforting. A glowing window may appear—offering ease and escape, asking nothing in return. But the longer the gaze lingers, the more the light fades elsewhere. Yet, even in the dimmest spaces, a stronger light can break through to restore.

But all things when they are exposed are made visible by light, for everything that is made visible is light. Therefore it says, "Wake up, sleeper, rise from the dead, and Christ will shine on you."

- Ephesians 5:13,14 (MSG)

Things aren't always what they seem.

From the outside, it looked beautiful—strong walls, warm lights, everything in its place.

The man who lived inside was a good man. Thoughtful. Capable. Faithful in the ways that gained the respect of others. No one would have guessed that deep inside the house, something was unraveling.

Most days, he moved through life with ease. He had built his home with care—one room for work, one for rest, one for prayer, one for laughter. But there were two rooms that defined him more than the others.

One he kept locked.

The other, he never meant to build at all.

The locked room sat at the end of a quiet hallway, barely noticeable unless you knew it was there. It had been there for years. He filled it slowly, over time, with things he didn't know how to deal with: small compromises, silent wounds, and fleeting temptations.

Later came the shame, regret, and lies.

Every time he passed the door, he felt their presence pressing through the wall. He told himself it was fine. As long as it stayed closed, the contents of the room couldn't hurt him. As long as the rest of the house stayed clean, he could keep being the man everyone needed him to be.

And then came the window.

He found it one night when he couldn't sleep. Restless and hollow, he wandered the halls until he noticed a soft glow coming from behind a door he didn't remember. Inside was a new room—bare, except for a tall, golden-framed window. It pulsed gently with light.

Curious, he stepped closer. He quickly realized it wasn't a window to the outside. It didn't look out toward the trees or sky or street. It looked into another world.

A world where shadows danced with shape and beauty. A world where no one asked questions. Where no one expected anything from him. Where eyes met his with wordless hunger and silent welcome. A world built for watching.

It didn't feel dangerous. Just... easy. So, he returned the following night. Then the next... and the next.

At first, it was a relief. A release. He told himself it was only a window, only a flicker of escape. He still prayed. Still served. Still meant well. He was still a good man. Just tired. Just worn. Just needing something to take the edge off.

But the window didn't satisfy. It numbed. And when the numbness wore off, the emptiness felt deeper. He returned, again and again, feeding a hunger that grew stronger the more he tried to silence it.

Soon, the rest of the house dimmed. The laughter in the kitchen faded. The comfort of the living room vanished. Even the hallway mirror no longer reflected his face with the same confidence.

He stopped opening the blinds. Stopped stepping outside. The window became enough. And then it became everything.

The more time he spent staring into that world, the less he wanted to live outside of it.

Friends reached out. He didn't answer.

Invitations came. He declined.

He didn't mean to become reclusive—but the shadows behind the glass always seemed easier than the mess of people, needs, and expectations.

Still, he returned. Not out of desire anymore, but desperation.

He began avoiding the rooms where people might ask how he was. He spent less time in the places where God had once felt near. He added more rooms—not for living, but for hiding. One for guilt, one for excuses, and one for silence.

He carefully built a double life, crafting a version of himself for others, while the shadows behind the window whispered to the one he tried to bury.

And the locked room? It groaned. The shame inside grew louder. The regrets clawed at the walls. The promises he kept breaking echoed off the ceiling.

He told himself he could stop.
That he would stop.
But he didn't.
Couldn't.
And that terrified him.

One night, as he stood before the glowing window, he noticed something he had never seen. A reflection. Not the shadows. Not the world on the other side. Him. Eyes hollow. Shoulders slumped. A man no longer whole.

And behind him... the locked room had opened. He hadn't touched it. But the door now stood wide.

He turned slowly and stepped inside.

It was worse than he imagined.

Darkness pressing in. Regret surrounded him like fog—heavy and inescapable. Names were written on the walls in his own hand:

Coward.
Addict.
Hypocrite.
Monster.
Fraud.

He dropped to his knees. Not because he was caught—but because he couldn't bear the weight of his failure anymore. He had tried to fight, to resist, and to fix himself. And he had lost... every single time.

And then—he heard a voice.

Not from the window and not from the shadows. It came from beyond the noise inside him.

It called his name.

Then, with quiet strength, it spoke a hope he hadn't dared feel in a long time.

"You don't have to face this alone."

It wasn't a voice of judgement or someone distant. It was the voice of someone who knew him. Someone who had seen behind every locked door, every glowing window, every compromise. And had never turned away.

"Give me your shame." The voice was steady, unshaken. *"Let me carry it for you."*

There was no anger in it. No accusation. Only the quiet ache of love that had waited a long time.

"You've been hiding for so long. Not because you love the dark—but because you've believed the light won't have you. But I am the light. And I have never stopped wanting you."

The words didn't demand change. They invited surrender. Not of behavior, but of the burden that had hardened his heart.

"Come into the light." The voice dropped to a whisper. *"Not to be exposed, but to be made whole."*

The words broke him open.

He wept—not just for his failures, but for the years he had tried to fight alone. For the lies he believed about being strong enough.

When his tears slowed, he realized his hands were open, empty, ready.

He stood—not because he felt strong, but because he no longer had to be.

He walked to the window one final time.

The glow still shimmered, and the shadows still moved.

But he no longer felt drawn to them. The temptation hadn't vanished—something greater had taken its place.

He reached for the curtain and pulled it shut.

The house fell silent. Not the silence of hiding—but the stillness of surrender.

He no longer felt alone.

This was the beginning of healing—a change that didn't start with behavior, but deep in the heart.

For only a changed heart can choose the light over the shadows.

THE FRIED CHICKEN

There's a quiet pressure that creeps in when we compare our-selves to others—especially when they seem newer, flashier, or more popular. We feel the need to add more, do more, become more—just to keep up or stay relevant. However, in that pursuit, we often lose the very thing that made us unique.

One handful of peaceful repose is better than two fistfuls of worried work—More spitting into the wind.

- Ecclesiastes 4:6 (MSG)

The little restaurant on the corner of Main and Maple had no flashing sign. No clever name. Just a hand-painted board above the door that read:

MAE'S FRIED CHICKEN.

The place was small—five booths, a creaky screen door, and the smell of cooking that made you feel like everything was going to be okay.

Mae—a silver-haired woman with smile lines, soft hands, and a flour-dusted apron—was known for one thing: fried chicken. Golden, crispy, and juicy. It always arrived at the table, still sizzling, with freshly mashed potatoes and baked cornbread, and a tall glass of sweet tea. That was the entire menu. It all fit easily on the chalkboard above the cash register.

And that was enough.

People came from miles around to sit at Mae's tables. Not for variety. But for the charm, the comfort, and the consistency.

Around town, Mae was a bit of a legend. People told stories about her chicken at backyard barbecues and church potlucks. A few local papers ran glowing articles. Tourists sometimes wandered off the highway just to get a seat, a plate, and a picture with Mae. Some even asked for her recipe. She never gave it out.

Mae's Fried Chicken wasn't just a restaurant—it was a memory in the making.

Then one day, a new restaurant opened down the street. Flashy. Trendy. All glass and neon. Their specialty was gourmet burgers and curated sauces—creations stacked high with names like *The Bourbon Beast* and *The Firecracker.*

People were curious. Lines formed. Phones came out. Hashtags flew.

At first, Mae didn't flinch. She kept her head down, her oil hot, and her chicken frying.

Then Friday lunch came and went with a quiet that settled too easily. On Saturday, she noticed a few empty chairs and no one waiting to be seated. The following week, the lunch crowd was even smaller.

Something shifted—not in the town, but in Mae. She tried to ignore it, but comparison has a way of slipping in through the back door. Even through the kitchen.

"*Maybe they want something different now.*" Mae's eyes swept over the empty tables, her voice carrying a trace of resignation.

"*Perhaps they're tired of chicken.*"

So, Mae added burgers to the menu.

Her kitchen wasn't designed for burgers, but she made it work. She even gave them names: *Mae's Maple Melt, Mae's BBQ Belt-buster,* and *Mae's Brisket Bonanza.*

And they sold, sort of. But not enough for her to feel better.

Then the burger place responded with a dessert bar—gelato, mini cakes, hand-torched s'mores. Their social media feeds exploded. Customers snapped selfies under twinkling lights and posted about the chef's creativity.

Mae bought a chocolate fountain.

She didn't even like chocolate that much.

"*It'll look good in the window,*" she said with a borrowed smile, as if she were trying to convince herself more than anyone else.

Then the new restaurant added special events: karaoke night, waffle Wednesdays, kids-eat-free hours. Feeling behind, Mae tried adding tacos and milkshakes.

The chalkboard menu grew crowded. The kitchen grew loud and hectic. Her small staff worked overtime trying to keep up. Mae started losing sleep.

And the chicken?

It started coming out rushed. A little too greasy. A little less magic. She no longer had time to wait for the oil to do its slow dance with the batter. She stopped singing to herself while she cooked. She stopped greeting customers by name.

And her hands—once soft and sure—started to tremble.

The competition grew fierce. Both restaurants ran themselves ragged trying to outdo each other. Mae couldn't tell if she was proud, panicked, or just plain tired. Each day brought a new idea, a new stress, a new reason to feel behind.

The town noticed. The charm faded. The comfort crumbled. The consistency was gone. What had once been unique became unrecognizable.

Soon, new food joints started popping up nearby. Trendier, younger, not as loyal. The buzz shifted, and the crowds moved on.

And eventually, both restaurants closed.

It was after a couple of years that Mae sat on a bench across the street, sipping a sweet tea, watching the sun cast shadows on the two empty buildings that used to feed a town. She stared at the faded sign that still bore her name.

The paint was chipped. The wood cracked from seasons of sun and rain. But the words were still there—plain, honest, and enough.

She let out a long sigh. She thought about the day she first opened—how she didn't worry about trends, tacos, or chocolate fountains.

A young woman passed with a little boy in hand. She stopped, turned, and called out:

"Are you... Mae?" The young woman's voice wavered between question and certainty, as if she already knew the answer.

Mae blinked, recognition flickering in her eyes. She gave a small nod. "Yes, I am."

The woman's face lit up. "*My dad brought me here every Saturday. He always said your chicken was the best thing he ever tasted.*"

She laughed softly, eyes shining. "*I can still hear the sizzle when you brought it to the table. Some of my best memories with him were over plates of your chicken.*"

Mae smiled at the thought of a once-little girl and her father enjoying a special moment in her restaurant. They lingered in remembrance and conversation for a few minutes.

Before long, the woman took her son's hand and continued down the street.

Mae's eyes followed them as they strolled away. Her lips quivered into a smile. She looked again at the building, and then at the sign over the door.

MAE'S FRIED CHICKEN.

The old sign had never changed. It never needed to.

She spoke softly to herself, almost as if confessing a secret:

"It *was always the chicken, Mae*," she said, a gentle reminder to her own heart.

Mae sat a little straighter on the weathered bench, as the late-afternoon sun warmed her shoulders. A soft breeze stirred, carrying the faint scent of frying oil that seemed to linger from years past.

Overhead, the sign creaked and swayed once... then twice, its faded letters shifting gently in the light. Mae watched it move, her breath catching for a moment. It felt less like wood and paint and more like a familiar voice...

... calling her back to where it all began.

THE INFINITE ROOMS OF INFINITE DOORS

We all live with the pressure of choices—what to pursue, what to leave behind, who to trust, and when to move. Every decision can feel like a door: some wide open, some barely cracked, and others locked tight. And behind each one lies the unknown. Over time, the weight of regret and fear of another misstep can make it hard to move at all. But what if the point was never to get every decision right? What if there's something—or someone—more trustworthy than the doors themselves, gently calling us forward?

"My sheep recognize my voice. I know them, and they follow me. I give them real and eternal life. They are protected from the Destroyer for good. No one can steal them from out of my hand."

- (Jesus) John 10:27,28 (MSG)

He woke in a hallway lined with doors.

Some thresholds stood wide open. Others stood barely cracked, just enough to tempt a glance. A few doors were locked. Or at least, they seemed that way—until he dared to push.

Most doors offered something: a path, a possibility, a promise.

Some shimmered with welcome. Others droned with quiet warning.

From some, voices beckoned: *"Come inside. This is what you've always wanted."*

From others came a sharp hiss in the dark: *"Don't even think about it."*

He listened. He waited. He weighed each one. And then eventually, he chose.

He stepped through a door.

The moment he crossed the threshold, the door behind him vanished—gone. No going back.

That was when the regret crept in. He thought about the doors he hadn't chosen, wondered what might have been. Some doors, he realized, he wished he'd never walked through. Others, he mourned, having missed them entirely.

The weight of it all felt like a cage. Not the room he stood in. Not the new doors surrounding him. But the choosing itself—that endless, gnawing burden of choice.

He hesitated longer with each door. He grew cautious. Fearful, even. Wounded by the memory of missteps and the echoes of voices that had lied. His own judgment had betrayed him before. Why trust it now?

But the rooms didn't stop. They never paused. They waited for no one.

Each new space carried the same feel—slightly different light, a shifting breeze, the faint echo of his own breathing. And always, more doors. Some opened to quiet, some to noise. Some to pain, others to fleeting peace. But he could never know which was which until he stepped through.

And none ever lasted.

Every step forward sealed something behind. Every choice left a shadow. And always—more rooms, more doors, stretching onward without end.

He tried to be smarter—to wait longer, to read the signs, to guess right, to avoid the pain. He once stopped before a single door for what felt like years, unsure if the pause was wisdom or only fear.

He spoke aloud once, just to see what it felt like. "Hello? Is anyone here?"

His voice carried into the silence. But the silence that answered was not empty. It was thick, as if the walls were listening.

He sank to the floor, his back against the wall. His eyes closed under the weight of all he hadn't said, hadn't done, hadn't chosen—and the heavier weight of all he had; the choices that led to disaster.

Just when fear held him tightest—when the ache of regret and the paralysis of uncertainty nearly anchored him to the floor—he heard it.

Not from the doors. Not from the room.

It was a voice that came from somewhere beyond, and somehow, also from within.

It simply spoke his name—with a familiarity that seemed to have always known him.

It knew every door he'd entered. Every one he hadn't. Every mistake. Every missed chance. Every locked room.

And still—it loved him.

"You were never meant to figure it all out on your own," the voice whispered, softer than a sigh. *"You were only asked to follow."*

He opened his eyes. Something in him broke. But not the breaking that ends things. The breaking that begins something new.

He realized he was never meant to master the maze. He was never created to wander the rooms alone. And he was certainly never meant to be defined by the doors he had chosen—or the ones he hadn't.

Because the one who called his name wasn't waiting at the last door—he was already here.

In every room. In every silence. In every decision yet to be made.

And still—he called.

He felt the voice as if it were kneeling beside him. Not rushing or pointing. Just waiting.

The man rose slowly—not because the path was clear, but because the voice was near.

He stepped toward a door—not the one that shimmered, not the one that hissed, but the one that felt... true.

He placed his hand on the handle. He didn't need certainty. He moved forward slowly. Not toward control. But toward trust.

Because the way was never just a destination. It was a presence—within and all around him.

THE HIGH-TECH GARDEN

We all want to grow something meaningful in our lives—something beautiful, lasting, alive. So we build systems. We strive for precision. We control what we can and adjust what we can't. But sometimes, despite all our effort, things still wilt. What if we cannot actually engineer the life we're working so hard to grow? What if what we need most is something we can't fabricate or manage, but something we have to trust?

Are you going to continue in this craziness? For only crazy people would think they could complete by their own efforts what was begun by God. If you weren't smart enough or strong enough to begin it, how do you suppose you could perfect it?

- Galatians 3:3 (MSG)

A young man planted a small garden behind his house. Just a patch of earth—nothing fancy. Just enough for something real.

He began with two rows of tomatoes. Waking early, he watered the plants by hand, weeding with a pocketknife and brushing dirt from the leaves with his fingertips. He trusted the sun to shine and the rain to fall. He didn't force results; he simply paid attention.

And it was enough.

The tomatoes came in fat and sweet, their skins splitting with ripeness. Neighbors leaned over the fence to admire them. Some even asked for seeds. The young man smiled at the compliments. He felt a little proud.

Maybe more than a little.

He planted more—peppers, cucumbers, a few herbs on the side.

When the work got harder, he built raised beds. Then he added drip lines to save time, a compost bin in the corner, an app to monitor soil moisture.

A quiet efficiency hummed in the once-simple garden. The rows were straight, the labels neat, and the settings optimized.

The neighbors still complimented his work, but their voices now carried a hint of awe—or was it distance?

No *matter*, he told himself. Everything was working. Every leaf, every root, right where he wanted it.

But then came a storm.

Wind tore the beds. Rain flooded the compost. Days of work were undone overnight.

It stung—more than he thought it should.

He added a canopy system to control the rain flow. Heating lamps for cold snaps. A fence to block out the rabbits. Security cameras to catch the squirrels.

He spent more time inside, adjusting dials and watching screens, than outside, touching leaves.

The garden still grew—technically. But something was different. The tomatoes looked perfect but tasted like water. The cucumbers were big but curled into strange shapes. The basil grew wild and bitter.

He told himself it was only a stage. "*I just need better settings,*" he said. "*Tighter schedules. More control.*"

He built more systems, fine-tuned the airflow, monitored the light angles, tweaked, twisted, tightened.

One morning, he stepped out and found the entire system... dead. The batteries had depleted, the sensors had gone dark, and the garden was silent—lifeless.

Across the fence, his neighbor—who had planted a lopsided garden using only seeds and a chipped watering can—was kneeling among her plants. There were no tarps or sensors—just her bare hands and a basket full of tomatoes, each one slightly bruised, uneven, and bursting with life.

She looked up and smiled. "*Want one?*" she offered, holding out a plump tomato.

He hesitated, then curiously reached for it. He examined the tomato. The skin was rough and the color uneven, but the first bite caught him off guard—sweet, messy, impossibly alive. The juice ran down his chin and onto his shirt.

He looked back at his own perfect rows of wilted vines, then down at the tomato in his hand. *"How did it come to this?"* he sighed to himself.

Taking off his gloves, he knelt in the dirt for the first time in years. He pressed his hands deep into the soil—it felt surprisingly satisfying.

Maybe what he and his garden needed most wasn't control—maybe it was trust.

He stayed there for a while, silent. The morning sun rose higher and higher as he watched his neighbor move from row to row with a kind of ease—not rushed, not precise, but focused on each plant.

Eventually, he stood, wiped his hands on his jeans, and turned back toward his house. But he didn't go inside. Not yet. He sat on the edge of the raised bed, the brittle vines behind him, and the bitten tomato in his hand.

"I can't believe I forgot what real fruit tastes like," he said in half-wonder.

His voice carried a note of wonder as he took another, bigger, juicy bite.

He didn't tear down all the high-tech systems that day. He didn't throw away the tools. But he left them untouched.

Instead, he walked next door and asked if he could help harvest—just for a little while, just to feel something living in his hands again.

"Start wherever you like," she said with a warm smile as she

handed him the basket.

And he did. Slowly, clumsily, like someone learning a language they used to speak.

He said little that day. But he returned the next morning. And the next.

When the next planting season came, he dug a new patch beside his old one—not as big, not as neat. No apps. No labels. No fences. No control.

Just a row of seeds and a watering can.

He wasn't sure how it would grow.

But this time, it didn't need to be perfect.

THE COOKING CLASS

There's a quiet shift that can happen when we spend too long focused on ourselves. Even the good things—growth, learning, healing—can slowly become centered on what we gain rather than what we can give. We tell ourselves we're preparing for something, but preparation without purpose turns inward. We protect what we've learned instead of sharing it. What happens when someone interrupts that inward posture and invites us to stop perfecting and start pouring out?

"Freely you have received; freely give."

- Jesus (Matthew 10:8b) NIV

At first, it was just something to do on Wednesday nights.

A flyer was pinned to a community center bulletin board:

LEARN TO COOK.
NO EXPERIENCE NEEDED.
SHOW UP HUNGRY.

And so they did.

Eight strangers gathered in a borrowed kitchen, each carrying their own quiet reason for showing up that first night: a retired nurse; a burned-out teacher; a college student tired of cereal; a night-shift worker who rarely spoke; a middle-aged man grieving his divorce; a recent widow learning how to live alone; and a couple of others who weren't sure why they'd come—only that they didn't want to face another dinner alone.

The instructor didn't make speeches—he simply handed out aprons, pointed to the ingredients, and let them begin.

They started with the basics—soups, stir-fries, pasta, roasted vegetables. Meals anyone could make, but somehow always tasted better when made together. Each week ended the same: they sat shoulder to shoulder around a long wooden table, passing plates, telling stories, laughing over burnt edges and celebrating the little victories. The food filled their stomachs. But the rhythm—the familiarity of chopping, stirring, connecting—filled something else.

By the seventh week, they'd become a quiet little family. Aprons were hung in the same spots. Knives laid out in familiar lines. They had inside jokes. Predictable roles. They didn't just know the recipes—they knew each other's stories.

Then the questions started.

"Are we going to move on to more advanced stuff?"

"I feel like I've kind of hit a ceiling."

"I love this, but... shouldn't we be learning more?"

The instructor grinned as if he knew a secret they didn't. "Bring your knives next week. We're going to do something different."

They arrived the following Wednesday evening expecting a new recipe, maybe a cooking challenge. Instead, they found crates of groceries—some fresh, some bruised—and stacks of plain take-out containers.

"What's this?" someone asked, blinking in confusion.

"There's a shelter across town," the instructor explained. "They're short on meals. So, tonight, we're cooking for them."

The room fell silent.

They looked at the ingredients. No recipe sheets. No polished produce. Just dented cans, wrinkled vegetables, bewilderment, and, inevitably, the commentary.

"But we're not trained for this."

"This isn't what I signed up for."

"I came here to learn."

"I'm not ready to cook for other people."

There were no raised voices, no dramatic exits—just the quiet, polite kind of resistance that doesn't look like rebellion—though it was. Two people slipped off their aprons and left. One offered a quick apology before going. The rest stood frozen, unsure.

A long pause stretched. The familiar warmth of the kitchen felt colder now. The absence of structure—no recipes, no instructions—left them exposed. They weren't students tonight. They were being asked to become something else.

Finally, one man stepped forward and grabbed an onion. Another turned on a burner. A third opened a can of beans and began improvising. Slowly, the room exhaled and came alive again—not in the same way as before, but with something new, something unfamiliar yet deeply purposeful.

That night, they packed over forty containers. Hearty, honest food. Nothing fancy. Just warm, filling, and real. A few of them volunteered to deliver the meals.

No one ate that night. No one complained.

At the shelter, they didn't know what to expect. They assumed they'd drop off the food and leave. But a volunteer waved them in.

"*Come see!*"

They hesitated—then followed.

They watched as people lined up, weary and quiet. A young mother helped her son cut his food into small bites. An older man closed his eyes before taking a bite. Shoulders dropped. Tension melted. A quiet dignity returned.

One student leaned closer to another and whispered, "I *never knew something this simple could matter so much.*"

The following week, the instructor gave them a choice.

"We can go back to recipes. Or we can keep cooking for them."

No one spoke for a moment. Then one hand lifted. Then another. Every hand in the room went up.

They cooked—week after week. The food got better. So did the teamwork.

They stopped worrying about technique and started imagining the people who would eat the meals—the hands that would hold the containers, the mouths that would taste the first bite. It changed the way they cooked. It changed why they cooked.

They started buying ingredients out of pocket, inviting friends to join, and hosting small fundraisers. Sometimes, they sat and ate with the guests at the shelter—not as rescuers, just as neighbors.

And then, one Wednesday, while cleaning up, an idea emerged.

"What if we didn't just bring food?" someone said, wiping their hands on a towel.

Heads turned.

"What if... we started a class?"

The idea grew in their voice.

"A class like ours—only here, at the shelter. For anyone who wants to learn. We'll bring the aprons. The knives. The time. And we'll teach them the way we were taught."

There was silence. Then slow nods. And something unspoken settled among them.

They had been fed. Now they were feeding.
They had been healed. Now they were helping.
They had learned. And now, they would teach.

What began as a class became a kitchen.
Then the kitchen became a community.
Then the community, a calling.

Without fanfare, they changed the world around them—one meal, one lesson, one life at a time.

THE SANCTUARY OF CERTAINTY

It's possible to spend a lifetime chasing answers and still miss what matters most. We can devote ourselves to learning, mastering ideas, even exploring the deepest questions about life and meaning—yet remain untouched, unchanged, and alone. Sometimes, the very things we use to seek truth become the things we hide behind. And sometimes, we must live the truth to truly understand it, not grasp it as an idea.

"You have your heads in your Bibles constantly because you think you'll find eternal life there. But you miss the forest for the trees. Thes Scriptures are all about me! And here I am, standing right before you, and you aren't willing to receive from me the life you say you want."

-Jesus (John 5:39,40) MSG

He believed he could explain almost every verse in the Bible—at least according to the one voice he trusted most: his own.

He lived on the edge of a university campus, in a weathered stone cottage beside an aging chapel.

Bookshelves sagged under the weight of thick volumes. Manuscripts crowded every drawer. Dog-eared commentaries lay open across the desk, margins scarred by his sharp handwriting. The coffee table was stained with the rings of long nights spent wrestling with sacred texts and questions that refused to rest.

He had spent his life learning ancient languages, diagramming syntax, and debating theology. The words of Scripture echoed in his mind like music—Greek and Hebrew, Latin and Aramaic—sounding like a symphony only he could hear.

He could unravel doctrine like a well-worn knot. He defended truth with the precision of a scalpel. And when doubt rose, he buried it beneath flawless logic.

His lectures were admired, his essays praised, and his mind celebrated for its depth.

And yet, the cottage was silent. No visitors. No laughter.

Only the scratching of his pen, the clicking of his laptop keyboard, and the echo of his own voice practicing arguments in empty rooms.

One afternoon, while studying a difficult passage about mercy, there was a knock at the door. Startled, he looked up—he had no appointments scheduled.

When he opened the door, a man stood there wearing worn jeans and a canvas satchel. His face bore the creases of sorrow, yet his eyes carried a quiet light. He looked like someone merely passing through. Too ordinary to draw attention. Too sensible to dismiss.

"*Peace to you, my friend,*" the visitor said.

"*Do I know you?*" The scholar lifted an eyebrow, puzzled.

"*You'd think so.*" The man smiled faintly. "*I've known you for a long time.*"

"*I rarely entertain visitors...*" The scholar hesitated, his voice cautious. "*I'm in the middle of something important.*"

"*So am I.*" The man's gaze didn't waver. "*May I come in?*"

"*Are you selling something? I'm not interested.*" The scholar shifted the door to close it.

The visitor didn't raise his voice. "*I am not here to sell. I have something for you. May I come in?*"

There was a long pause.

The scholar eased the door back open and stepped aside, motioning toward the wooden chair across from his desk.

The man entered, his eyes drifting over the room before he sat.

"*You spend your days with sacred words,*" the man observed.

"I do," the scholar replied as he settled into the big chair behind his desk.

"*You study to find the heart of God.*"

"Yes," the scholar said, straightening his posture with pride. "*I've given my life to that pursuit.*"

"*Have you found it?*" the visitor asked.

The scholar blinked, surprised.

"What kind of question is that?" His tone sharpened. *"I've devoted my entire life to Scripture. I've studied the original languages, traced the patterns, uncovered the layers of meaning."*

He gestured toward the open books on his desk. *"Of course I've 'found it.'"*

But even as the words left his mouth, something about them rang hollow.

The visitor nodded slowly.

"And when did you last sit with someone whose world was falling apart?"

The scholar's eyes drifted to the shelves, avoiding his visitor's gaze.

"That's not my role. I'm not a counselor." He lifted the book with his name on the cover. *"I lead with ideas. Others carry them out."*

"And do they?" The visitor's question carried no accusation—only curiosity.

The words struck harder than the scholar expected.

For a moment, he hesitated. He had never really asked himself that. His expression stayed composed.

"That's not for me to measure," he said quickly, his tone thinning. *"My task is to illuminate the truth. What others do with it... is their responsibility."*

But his voice had lost a shade of its former certainty.

His jaw tightened. "*Without truth, action is misguided.*"

The visitor leaned forward slightly. "*And without love, truth becomes a shield to hide behind.*"

The scholar's shoulders stiffened; he masked it with a thin, dismissive laugh.

"*I think you may be out of your depth in this conversation.*"

But the visitor didn't blink. He held the scholar's gaze—not in defiance or judgment, but with a stillness that felt ancient.

"*I was hungry, and you annotated a text.*
I was grieving, and you offered a lecture.
I was a stranger, and you questioned my theology."

A strange chill passed through the room.

The scholar shifted in his chair, unsettled.

There was something familiar about the man on the other side of his desk—something hard to define, like memory and prophecy mingled together. A whisper stirred in the back of his mind, the distant echo of a verse he could almost remember.

"*You speak as if...*" His words caught in his throat.

"*Your mind overflows with truth,*" the visitor sighed, "*but your heart... your heart has become parched.*"

He rose from his wooden chair and turned toward the door.

"*Wait.*" The scholar stood up quickly.

The man turned back. Sorrow etched his face, but his eyes held something unshakable—recognition, perhaps, or grace. Something beyond human, yet clothed in humility.

"*You search the Scriptures,*" he said softly, "*thinking they give you life. But they point to me. Still... you've never come.*"

The scholar's knees faltered.

The visitor reached for the door, then paused. Turning, he offered a faint smile and put his hand on the scholar's shoulder.

"*There's a difference between knowing about me... and knowing me.*"

He stepped into the night and was gone.

The scholar stood frozen in the doorway, desperate to make sense of what had just happened.

The cottage, once a sanctuary of certainty, suddenly felt different. Not wrong—just incomplete.

That night, the scholar left his books closed. He opened the window. He sat in stillness and listened for the life around him.

The chapel bell rang—a sound he hadn't noticed in years—returning to him with startling clarity.

The next morning, he walked into town—bread under his arm for a widow.

He lingered with a man who carried the scent of loss.

He helped a young girl hunt for her missing dog.

He still studied. He still wrote. But his ink was now mixed with tears of thankfulness. He asked fewer questions to prove a point and more to understand a person.

Truth, he realized, was still vital—but it now had a face and a voice.

And every evening, he left the door unlocked—a small ritual to remind him...

... that his home was never closed to a stranger.

THE OPEN LEDGER

Some wounds don't fade with time. We carry them—quietly, sometimes proudly—believing we're protecting ourselves. Sometimes, we even hold them like leverage, proof that someone still owes us something. But what if holding on is the very thing keeping us stuck? What if the freedom we long for only begins the moment we choose to release what was never ours to carry to begin with?

"In prayer there is a connection between what God does and what you do. You can't get forgiveness from God, for instance, without also forgiving others. If you refuse to do your part, you cut yourself off from God's part."

(Jesus) Matthew 16:14,15 (MSG)

She carried a ledger everywhere she went.

Not of the financial kind, though it looked like one—small, no larger than a paperback book, but thick with pages that had swelled with time. The leather cover was stiff and scuffed—years of opening and closing had worn the zipper smooth. Tucked into the spine was a refillable silver pen.

The pages inside weren't numbered, but the names were. Some written large, others in small, resentful script. Some circled. Some underlined. A few names were stained—a fallen tear perhaps, from long ago.

Next to each name were dates, memories, and phrases that replayed like old voicemails: a word too sharp, a silence too long, a kindness withheld at the wrong time, missed birthdays, bitter glances, invitations that never came, words spoken behind her back—or worse, words never spoken at all.

It wasn't for business. It wasn't for healing. It was for remembering.

She called it honesty. Others—if they dared—might have called it something else: resentment, maybe even revenge. But no one challenged her. She was too composed. Too articulate. Too justified. She always had the facts. Her entries were exact, down to the tone of a voice, the pause in a sentence, the timestamp of a message never replied to.

At first, the ledger gave her strength. She could control the narrative. Hold people accountable—even if they never knew it. Each new entry gave her a strange sense of power. Protection, she told herself. If she remembered the pain, she wouldn't be caught off guard again. Documenting the hurt would protect her from being wounded twice by the same person.

The ledger grew thick... and so did her heart.

She smiled less. Laughed less. Trusted less. Even the innocent had to prove themselves now. The book had become her lens. Everyone was guilty until proven pure. No one ever was.

She used to love people. Now she studied them.

On a rainy evening, she sat alone at her usual café. The place was mostly empty. The only sounds were the hush of voices at other tables—soft, slow, and just out of reach. She stared out the window—the ledger closed but near, her hand resting protectively over it.

A man approached her table.

"*Mind if I sit?*" His voice was polite but intentional, as if she were the reason he was there.

She looked around the café, a quiet signal that plenty of other seats were available. But something in his tone—not entitled, not casual, just sincere—made her think: *Why not?*

He noticed the ledger. She could tell. Most people didn't.

He didn't ask about it. He just placed a smaller book of his own on the table. The leather cover was cracked. The corners frayed.

"*I carry one too,*" he said.

Her eyes narrowed. "*Really?*" she asked, her voice low, clipped, guarded.

He slid it toward her. She opened it cautiously, not sure why her hands trembled slightly.

There was only one name inside: hers.

Just one line beside it: *Forgiven. As she forgives.*

She stared at it, reading the words over and over. They didn't make sense—or maybe they made too much sense.

"What's that supposed to mean?" she asked, her voice catching on the edge of disbelief.

He met her eyes—not smug, not sharp, just steady.

"It means," he said, *"the measure you use is the one used to measure you."*

Her chest tightened. She looked down at her ledger: the names, the accusations, the betrayals—all perfectly chronicled, pages and pages of it.

"But," she whispered, *"they were wrong. They hurt me."*

"I know," his voice was tender, like a father comforting a child after a hard fall.

She leaned in, her words forced through her whisper, but carrying the weight of a shout.

"I have a right to be angry!" She clenched her fists on the table.*" You don't know what they did... what it cost me"*

Though her words flared with anger, his gaze gentled, and his voice held its quiet composure.

"You do. You have every right. But holding onto your right won't heal what someone has broken. It'll only keep you bound to it."

She looked down at her open ledger.

"They never even said they were sorry."

"*I know.*"

She looked away, eyes fixed on nothing in particular. She folded her arms tightly across her chest. When she finally spoke, her voice cracked.

"So *what happens if I can't let go?*"

He was silent for a long moment before speaking, his words carrying a sorrow older than the book he had laid on the table.

He was silent for a long moment before speaking again.

"*Then that's what's written next to your name.*"

She looked at the open ledgers, then reached out and slammed them both shut.

Silence stretched between them.

Outside, the crosswalk light changed. A car passed. A child laughed two tables over.

Almost without realizing it, she reached for her ledger. She stared at the name at the top of the page. It wasn't the worst entry—just the one that had lived there the longest. Her pen hovered, then slipped from her fingers. She tore the page out. Folded it once. Then again. She dropped it into the empty coffee cup in front of her.

The man didn't react. He didn't need to.

She turned the page—another name, another wound.

This one took longer. She read the entry again and again, re-membering the moment it had happened. The pain was real. Still tender.

Tears formed in the wells of her eyes. But she tore the page out too.

She didn't finish that night. Or even that month. Some pages were more difficult to read than others. Some reopened wounds she'd thought had long healed. Some entries made her hands shake.

But she kept going.

And somewhere near the end, she began to understand—really understand—that the book she held against others had become the book being held for her.

The ledger wasn't just a weight—it was a mirror. And the freedom she longed for wasn't in being proven right.

It came when she loosened her grip and let the flow of grace return.

THE FISHING BARRELS

Some stories are so familiar, we stop questioning them. We grow up learning how to succeed, how to compare, how to win. We learn to chase what others call important, but we seldom stop to ask why. This story isn't about fishing. It's about what happens when we spend our lives competing inside small spaces—barrels we didn't even realize we were in—while missing the invitation to something far more wild, beautiful, and free.

"Come with me. I'll make a new kind of fisherman out of you."

-(Jesus) Matthew 4:19 (MSG)

Two boys stood on the shoreline, each beside a wooden barrel filled with water.

The two barrels were small—big enough to hold a handful of silver fish that darted and swirled in lazy circles. The sun caught on their scales, turning them into little flashes of light with every turn.

Each boy gripped a fishing rod, its line dangling into the other's barrels. They cast and pulled with practiced ease, laughter breaking out whenever one made a catch.

"*I got another one!*" the first boy shouted, holding up a wriggling fish that flicked saltwater onto his shirt. He transferred it into his barrel with a splash.

The second boy narrowed his eyes and cast quickly.

"*Not for long.*"

Moments later, he hooked the same fish and dropped it back into his own barrel with a victorious grin.

Back and forth they went.

Cast.
Catch.
Transfer.
Celebrate.

But then the first boy got an idea.

One morning he appeared on the beach carrying a brand-new fishing rod, longer and sleeker than the one before. Its reel gleamed in the sunlight, and the line cut through the air with a satisfying swish.

"Look *at this beauty.*" His eyes sparkled as he held it up. "*It'll catch fish twice as fast.*"

The second boy frowned at his older rod. Not wanting to be outdone, he set off down the beach and returned later with a small pouch filled with different bait—colorful and expensive.

"*Your rod might be fancy,*" he said, lifting the pouch, "*but watch how they go for my bait.*"

They cast into the barrels again. The first boy marveled at how smoothly his new rod worked, while the second boasted that his bait was irresistible.

Back and forth they went, stealing from each other's barrel, even more determined to out-fish one another.

But the barrels never grew fuller. The fish never grew stronger. Yet the friendly rivalry made the game feel alive.

People strolled along the beach now and then, slowing as they passed the boys, watching the odd scene unfold. A few smirked, whispering to each other and shaking their heads in quiet disbelief.

"*They're fishing from barrels,*" one said.

"*Why don't they turn around?*" another asked.

But the boys didn't hear them. Their laughter rang out across the beach, their eyes fixed on the barrels—small, contained, safe.

Behind them, the ocean stretched to the horizon. It glittered under the sunlight, its surface broken now and then by schools of fish leaping and swirling—thousands of them. The air smelled of salt and possibility, the sound of breaking waves like an unending invitation.

But neither boy turned.

The first boy adjusted his stance, rod bent as he wrestled with another catch.

"*This one's mine now.*" His grin widened as he pulled.

The second boy scowled. "*You're just jealous my barrel's better.*"

"*Better?*" The first boy laughed. "*It's got all my fish in it!*"

Their teasing went back and forth, but they never took their eyes off the barrels.

A fish leapt from the ocean behind them, catching the sun on its scales like liquid flame. It arced high before vanishing into the waves with a soft splash.

The boys didn't notice.

The older boy dropped his line into the barrel. It snagged immediately. He tugged hard, determined to wrestle his prize free. The fish thrashed, water splashing over the barrel's edge.

"*This one's a fighter.*" His jaw tightened as he reeled it in.

"*Careful.*" The younger boy's eyes widened. "*You'll tire them out.*"

With a final yank, he pulled it out. The fish flopped weakly as it dropped into the barrel.

For a moment, neither spoke.

The ocean's voice grew louder now—the thumping of its waves folding over one another, gulls crying in the distance.

The younger boy's eyes flicked toward the sound. He squinted at the horizon, where the sun touched the water like a golden flame.

"*Do you ever wonder...*" his words hung in the air.

"*Wonder what?*" the older boy asked, not looking up.

"*What's out there... in the big water?*"

The older boy didn't look up. He re-baited his hook, frowning.

"*Don't be stupid. It's dangerous out there. You can't even see the bottom.*"

"*But maybe we could catch more fish.*"

The older boy laughed. "*More fish? I've got all I need right here.*" He patted the side of his barrel with pride. "*So do you.*"

The younger boy nodded slowly, but his eyes lingered on the waves. For the first time, he noticed movement—schools of fish just beneath the surface, shimmering in patterns too beautiful to describe.

"*What if...*" he said softly. "*What if we're fishing in the wrong place?*"

The older boy's head snapped up. "*Don't start that. This is so much better.*"

"*Why is this better than out there?*" the young boy pressed.

But the older boy's glare held him. "*Because this way, we can tell everyone we always catch a lot of fish.*"

The younger one nodded and cast his line once again into his friend's barrel.

And so they went on for the rest of the day.

Cast.
Catch.
Transfer.
Celebrate.

Behind them, the ocean rolled in ceaselessly—one wave chasing the next, each heavy with immeasurable promise.

THE FITTING ROOM

Identity can feel like something we have to define, defend, or display. But beneath the surface, there's often a deeper question: What if the ache we carry isn't about finding the right label—but being known by the right source?

Christ's life showed me how, and enabled me to do it. I identified myself completely with him. Indeed, I have been crucified with Christ.

-Galatians 2:20 (MSG)

He hadn't come looking for answers.

He came because nothing he tried on ever felt right—not the labels, not the roles, not even the freedom to choose. He never felt as though he had chosen any of it. The feelings were simply there—unasked for, unshakable, sometimes loud, sometimes whispering.

First came the questions. Then the labels. Then the hope that one of them would finally make him feel whole.

He had tried identifying as straight—because that's what he was told was normal. Then gay—because that finally felt honest. Then something in between—because even that didn't explain everything inside him. He wore each piece like a carefully designed outfit, hoping one would finally fit and feel... enough.

Some identities gave him confidence. Others offered him community. But none of them gave him peace.

Every mirror left him with the same ache: *Why do I still feel unknown—even to myself?*

He wasn't angry with God. He just didn't know where God fit into all this. Everyone else seemed so confident—some shouting verses, others shouting pride. He just wanted to breathe.

That's when someone told him about the shop. Not an actual shop, not exactly—more like a place you only find when you're ready or when you're finally too tired to perform.

There were no signs, no loud promises—just a door that stuck a little when you opened it and a bell that rang too softly to notice. Inside were racks of clothes—every possible style, every possible identity. Not just sexual or gender identities, but *success* and *significance, image* and *influence*—even *pain, protection, and pride*. Every piece had seen prior wear. Each one promised to say something true about who he was.

He walked through the rows slowly. He'd seen all of this before: labels that promised to make him feel strong, or safe, or like he finally belonged.

Try this one—you'll feel seen.

Try this one—you'll feel powerful.

Try this one—nothing will ever hurt you again.

Try this one—you'll finally belong.

But in the very back, behind a faded curtain, was a room with no mirror. Just a bench, soft lighting, and a folded piece of clothing that looked too plain to be of value. Next to it lay a handwritten note:

This won't fix your feelings.
This won't erase your past.
And this won't make the questions go away.
But if you're willing to surrender every identity you've carried—
I will give you one that can never be taken from you.

He sat for a long time. Not because he was ashamed, but because he had worked so hard to build something—to be something—and now he wasn't even sure what that something was anymore.

He thought the problem was his attractions. Or his behavior.

Or the way people looked at him—too curious or too quiet. But sitting there in the stillness, he sensed something deeper—a whisper beneath all the noise.

The deeper question wasn't "Who am I attracted to?" It was "Who can tell me who I really am?"

And then, almost like it had been waiting for him to stop striving, another question surfaced:

"What if my identity is deeper than who I'm attracted to?"

Maybe it wasn't about orientation or expression, or about finding a label that finally fit. What if it had always been about his heart?

He had spent years trying to name himself—not because he chose his desires, but because he thought his desires had already chosen him. He shaped his entire identity around what he felt, what he feared, and what he hoped might finally bring him peace.

What if identity isn't something you declare—but something you receive?

He remembered how tired he felt—worn thin by every attempt to be understood by his family, by others, by himself, even by God. And now he saw it all for what it was: not rebellion or confusion, but longing—the longing to be known. Fully known. Beyond the categories, the arguments, and the fear.

With trembling hands, he reached for the plain garment. But before he could put it on, he noticed how heavy the clothes he wore had become—layer after layer of labels and expectations, stitched tight with fear and shame.

One by one, he slipped them off—the garments of performance, the jackets of pride, the scarves of regret. Each one felt heavier than he remembered. When the last of them fell to the floor, he stood there—lighter, yet more exposed than ever.

Then he picked up the plain garment. It didn't look impressive, make a statement, or even carry a label. But the moment he pulled it over his head, he didn't feel erased—he felt anchored. Anchored not just to who he was, but to something truer, something unshakable.

He didn't walk out straight. He didn't walk out fixed. But he walked out surrendered—lighter, as if he'd set down a burden too heavy to name. And in that surrender, he found something stronger—stronger than certainty, stronger than desire, stronger than fear.

He found peace, not because he had figured out who he was, but because he had let go...

... and trusted the One whose identity would never change.

THE TERMINATED COWORKER

Judgement often disguises itself as justice. We shake our heads, pass along a story, and feel better about ourselves because someone else got caught. But underneath the headlines and hushed-toned conversations is a harder truth: most downfalls don't begin with scandal—they start with small compromises that no one sees. What if the line between right and wrong isn't as far from us as we think?

"Don't pick on people, jump on their failures, criticize their faults—unless, of course, you want the same treatment. Don't condemn those who are down; that hardness can boomerang. Be easy on people; you'll find life a lot easier."

- (Jesus) Luke 6:37 (MSG)

He wasn't even out of the parking lot before the commentary began—thinly veiled judgment spoken just loud enough to be heard, as if watching through glass made them innocent.

The management didn't use his name. The email only said that someone was no longer with the company. "*Violation of policy,*" they called it—cold, clipped, and vague enough to meet HR standards. But no one needed the name. Everyone already knew who it was.

The whispers had been circulating for days: personal expenses charged to the company card; falsified reports; a pattern of little lies that eventually caught up with him.

It wasn't just the money. It was a breach of trust. He held a position of influence. Others had looked up to him. Now HR had to keep things tight—legal implications, damaged credibility, internal audits. The official language stayed vague on purpose, but behind the scenes the impact was clear. Trust had been shattered like a dropped mug no one wanted to claim.

After the all-hands meeting ended, a few people lingered in the conference room. The door stayed open, but the air inside felt sealed. Laptops were closed, coffee cups pushed aside. A few stood by the window, watching through the blinds as he walked to his car—slow, deliberate, carrying a cardboard box of personal items.

One man crossed his arms, still staring through the slats. "*He brought it on himself.*" The words came out flat, without him looking away. "*You lie to the company, you lose your job. Simple as that.*"

Another voice joined in. "*He always had that 'trust me' vibe. Turns out he was just really good at faking it.*"

There was no outrage in the room—just a strange satisfaction, an unspoken feeling of being on the safer side of someone else's downfall. A sense of relief that it hadn't been them. It was easier to process the situation by assigning blame than by facing what it stirred in themselves.

Then a young woman at the table, quiet until now, spoke—calm, deliberate. "*Funny how easy it is to talk like we'd never do the same.*"

The room didn't move. The blinds clicked softly as someone let them fall shut.

She scanned the faces in the room, but most looked away. "*We act like he's some kind of con artist. But if someone pulled the receipts from our own lives—how many of us would still be here? What about the corners we've cut? The things we've justified? The money we borrowed without asking? The hours we claimed we worked but didn't?*"

A scoff came from the far end of the room. "*Yeah, but slipping up isn't the same as fraud.*"

The woman stood up and walked to the water cooler. She filled her paper cup, took a sip, then turned and faced the room. "*I've taken shortcuts I didn't admit to. I've manipulated numbers to make the report look better. I've stated I was working when I wasn't. I've told myself it wasn't a big deal because no one noticed.*"

No one replied.

One person stared at their phone. Another picked at the edge of a napkin, as if it held the answer. Someone else glanced toward the door, hoping for an easy exit from the moment. The silence that followed wasn't empty—it was dense, like a fog had crept into the room.

The woman felt the weight of the moment and kept going. "We *think falling is the moment you get caught, but most people fall long before that—in small, invisible ways. That's where it starts. Where our character gets shaped... or lost."*

Still, no one pushed back. No clever one-liners. No corrections. The room wasn't hostile—just quiet. Tense. Reflective, even. The young woman sensed this was her chance to say something real—something that mattered.

"I'm not saying what he did was okay." She lowered her eyes and shook her head. *"It wasn't. But judging him doesn't make us clean—it just makes us feel safer... superior. It makes us forget how close we all live to that line.*

Another silence came—this one heavier.

The unspoken thoughts in the room no longer lingered on the coworker they'd seen escorted from the building. Now it was about themselves: their habits, their hidden compromises, the parts of their lives that might not hold up if the light shifted just slightly.

And for the first time—maybe ever—the realization that none of them were untouchable became real.

A chair scraped. Someone cleared his throat. A half-eaten muffin was quietly tossed into the trash. Eventually, they started gathering their things. No one said much—just a few comments about needing to get back to work. They filed out one by one, avoiding eye contact, each carrying more weight than when they'd entered.

The last person sat for a few extra seconds, staring at the closed blinds. He never spoke the entire time, hadn't nodded, nor flinched. But something had settled over him—a new clarity.

It wasn't guilt, but awareness. The sobering recognition of what he, too, was capable of. The realization that his reputation had become a kind of armor. And if that armor cracked even slightly, he wondered...

... Who would still be there for me?

THE HOUSE OF WONDER

Some places are so familiar we stop noticing them. Patterns repeat until they blend into the background. But wonder—true, mouth-dropping awe—doesn't live in what we already know. It waits just beyond the edge of the familiar, where the curtain of the ordinary lifts and the sacred is revealed. There, in the stillness beyond certainty, awe unfolds into wisdom.

The fear of the Lord is the beginning of wisdom, and knowledge of the Holy One is understanding.

- Proverbs 9:10 (NIV)

She had spent her whole life inside the House.

Some corridors unfolded into quiet galleries. Staircases spiraled upward into silence, and windows opened to horizons so wide they felt unmeasured.

All who lived within called it "*the House.*"

She grew up tracing its patterns and passages—the secret corners where one could disappear and the warm places where one could be found. She knew how the pipes hummed just before the heat arrived, the sweet drift from the baking room, the hollow knock of shoes on the old wooden floors. She even knew the slow rhythm of sunlight as it crossed the rooms, rising and falling like a gentle tide.

The House had taught her more than any book or teacher.

It shaped her habits and soothed her fears. It became the measure of her world. In truth, the House was her entire world.

Most days, she wandered freely and with little thought—comfortable, predictable, and safe.

Then came the day she noticed the tapestry.

It wasn't new to her. She had passed it hundreds of times—a threadbare cloth, hanging limp against the wall, stretching from ceiling to floor. So familiar and faded that, after all this time, it had almost become part of the wall—invisible.

But on this day, a stray breeze drifted through the corridor, stirring the fabric—not wildly, not loudly, but just enough to catch her eye. It swayed slowly, almost deliberately, as if beckoning her closer.

She paused, then reached for the cloth. It was heavier than she expected. She had to tug hard, using both hands to lift the bottom corner away from the wall and make room to see behind it.

That's when she saw the door. *How had she never noticed it before?*

She slipped behind the tapestry and laid her hand on the brass knob. It turned easily. The hinges of the door groaned like a voice clearing its throat after years of silence.

A narrow staircase led upward, leaving behind the light of the room she was in.

She hesitated. Just long enough to know this was different. The air didn't smell musty or stale. It was fresh, like the first day of spring.

She placed her foot on the first step and froze, waiting for something—anything. The air seemed to hold its breath. No crack of wood beneath her. No hidden voice calling her back. Only silence.

She stepped forward, deciding to follow wherever the stairs might lead. With each step, she felt her heartbeat quicken—not from fear, but from something close to it.

Maybe it was anticipation, adventure, or perhaps even reverence. As she climbed, the atmosphere seemed to change—growing thinner, cooler, sharper with each step.

The stairs turned and narrowed. The light dimmed further. Her fingers traced the cool stone walls as she climbed. She wondered how far the stairs extended and whether anyone had traveled this way before. But she kept climbing.

STEVEN L. BARR

At the top waited another door—unlocked, as if expecting her. She pushed it open, and a flood of white-gold light poured in, spilling across the threshold as the door swung wide. She stepped through, blinking against the brilliance, and emerged onto the roof.

There she stood, breath caught in her throat, as for the first time she saw the House—no longer from within, but rising in its full vastness before her, beneath her, and beyond her.

She staggered slightly, her breath caught in her throat. It was not just large—it was limitless. Towers and wings and archways shimmered in the light, stretching out toward the horizon. The shingles beneath her feet gleamed like stone and fire.

She turned slowly, trying to take it all in. She had spent her whole life within these walls. She knew the sound of every opening door, the feel of its carpets, the echo of its staircases.

But here—on the roof—it was as if she had never known the House at all.

And in that moment, she felt it—a trembling. Not the kind that arises from danger or dread, but from the realization that you are in the presence of something immeasurably greater than yourself.

The sight stole her breath, and her knees gave way until she found herself sitting.

For a long moment she stayed where she landed, gathering her bearings. Then, drawn by the view, she edged forward and lowered herself to the roof's rim, legs dangling freely over the open expanse—astonished, but unafraid.

Overwhelmed, she leaned forward slightly, unafraid, letting the breeze brush her face as she took in the endless view.

For a long moment, she stayed that way—silent, heart pounding, soul stilled by the sheer immensity of what surrounded her.

She felt so small, so humbled, so awestruck. And she had never felt so alive.

A strong wind rose over the roof. The whisper settled over her as if with unseen hands—resting gently on her shoulders, both tender and commanding.

"And this is only what you can see," the whisper came, calm and close, as if it had been waiting all along.

Her eyes stung as the words settled in. She blinked, trying to clear the blur, then blinked again, but the sting remained—part wonder, part something she couldn't yet name.

How small she felt to think this was the end—to imagine that this vast and beautiful moment could contain the fullness of what had built the House.

She thought about the rooms she had passed without noticing. The corridors she had rushed through without reverence. How many moments of wonder had she missed while believing she already knew everything there was to see?

She thought about the people who had never even found the stairs. They assumed the House was only what could be touched or measured.

What would happen if she told them about this place—about the view that stretched beyond everything they thought they knew? Would they believe her, or laugh it off as a dream? Would they dare to climb, step by step, into the unknown, or stay where the familiar walls felt safer?

She sat there for a long time. Not because she was afraid to leave, but because she knew everything would be different from now on. She would never walk the halls beneath her the same way again.

The rooms she once thought were ordinary revealed themselves as sacred. The sounds she once took for granted now rose like quiet songs.

And the trembling she felt deep in her bones did not drive her away; it made her listen, it made her wonder...

... and in time, it made her wise.

THE CUPPA JOE

There's a quiet pull in all of us toward the way things used to be. Nostalgia can feel like comfort, even safety. But the world doesn't stop moving, and sometimes the hardest part of growing is realizing that what once gave life might now hold it back. It takes courage to let go of what's familiar in order to make space for what's possible. And sometimes, the very thing we fear losing is the thing that needs to be released in order to thrive.

"And you don't put wine in old, cracked bottles; you get strong, clean bottles for your fresh vintage wine."

- (Jesus) Luke 5:37,38 (MSG)

The coffee shop was called *The Cuppa Joe*.

It was nestled between a dusty bookstore and a dry cleaner with an awning that had faded from red to salmon pink. It had been around for decades—one of those places where time seemed to slow. Polaroids and vintage posters covered the walls. The chairs were a mismatched collection. The Wi-Fi was spotty... when it worked. And the coffee, brewed in clunky silver pots, tasted less of beans and more of memory.

The owner who ran the place had opened it back when cassette tapes were still in glove compartments and people still read newspapers. He was nearly always in flannel, as if reminding himself—and everyone else—that comfort had always mattered more than polish. The dream was simple: to create a space where people didn't just consume—they connected.

Once, there were plans for poetry nights, long tables, and a second location. But over time, the dream settled into a rhythm. The rhythm became routine—and routines often become ruts.

But the regulars loved it.

"Feels like stepping back in time," an older man said, cradling a drip roast that hadn't changed in thirty years. *"You don't find places like this anymore."*

He traced a slow circle on the table with his finger. *"There used to be an ashtray right here."* He stared at the empty spot as if it might reappear, then gave a couple of half-hearted coughs. *"I miss those days."*

The regulars meant it as praise. The owner received like gospel.

The leaning chalkboard menu had seen much better days. There was no espresso machine, no syrups, and definitely no oat milk.

You never saw laptops, apps, or earbuds.

"This is the kind of place real coffee shops used to be—before the world got too busy," the owner often said.

But the city changed. The street filled with fresh faces. The dry cleaner next door became a co-working space. The bookstore on the other side went out of business, replaced by a high-end juice bar. And while young professionals walked past with their phones and podcasts and soy lattes, The Cuppa Joe remained exactly the same.

One day, someone much younger walked in—eyes scanning the room.

"This place is incredible," he said. *"But it feels... I don't know... stuck. Have you ever thought about updating it?"*

The owner didn't hesitate. *"Why mess with what works?"*

Then came the pause. *"But does it still work?"* the new customer asked.

The owner had never given it much thought.

Over time, the regulars had aged. Many had passed away. New faces were few and far between.

Yet, change felt like betrayal. The shop had become a keeper of memories—first dates, farewell hugs, hard conversations, forgiveness, laughter, grief. Letting it change felt like letting go of what made those memories sacred.

One cold morning, the radiator gave out. Steam hissed like a warning. Pipes clanked like old bones. Then, with one last groan, the plumbing gave way.

The mop wasn't enough. Water had soaked the floorboards. The smell of old wood, damp plaster, and mold filled the air.

A surprising question stirred in the owner's mind, soft but unrelenting:

Have I been holding on to something that's become an empty shell?

Later that night, alone in the wreckage, he opened a drawer beneath the counter. Inside were old paper notes, forgotten suggestion cards, and napkin doodles.

One note stood out. It was faded and written in a youthful hand.

At *The Cuppa Joe*,
everyone should always
feel seen, welcomed, and loved.

The note wasn't from a stranger. It was in the owner's handwriting. This was the original dream. And that's when it became clear.

The goal was never to keep things the same. It had never been about the method. It was about the mission.

The next morning, the owner locked the door for the last time, then taped a paper sign to the glass, pressing it flat:.

This chapter is closing.
But something new is brewing.
Stay tuned.

Three months later, across town, a small Airstream trailer gleamed beneath string lights beside a mural wall. Warm-colored letters adorned the side of the trailer, spelling out **The Cuppa Joe**.

There was no cash register. Customers were simply asked to *"pay-what-you-can."* There was no fixed menu, just rotating drinks created by local baristas. Long tables with mismatched benches replaced chairs.

On Thursday nights, a makeshift sound system and a tiny stage were provided—for stories, prayers, laughter, and songs.

Inside the trailer window, stood the same flannel shirt. But the heart inside it had changed. He was no longer trying to relive the past. Now he was choosing to trust the future.

People came. Not just the old regulars, but artists, seekers, skeptics, and students. Those who knew where to find grace in a place that served warmth without conditions.

The dream had not been lost.
It had been re-filled.

THE FOLDED NAPKINS

Some people are easy to miss. They don't hold titles, lead meetings, or stand in the spotlight. But that doesn't mean they aren't part of something bigger. Again and again, God works through the quiet ones—the ones others overlook or ignore—to remind us who really holds the power. Not the experts. Not the impressive. But the One who sees what others don't.

Isn't it obvious that God deliberately chose men and women that the culture overlooks and exploits and abuses, chose these "nobodies" to expose the hollow pretensions of the "somebodies?"

-1 Corinthians 1:27 (MSG)

The hospital had everything. State-of-the-art machines. World-renowned doctors. Research grants. A lobby with fresh orchids changed every Monday. It was the kind of place where hope wore lab coats and diagnoses came wrapped in careful, clinical words.

But still—one child would not speak.

She had been in the pediatric ward for nearly three months. A brain injury had stolen her words, leaving her trapped in silence. The doctors spoke cautiously of therapy and treatment, of fragile pathways in the brain that might awaken again. The odds were against her, but there was always hope. Her voice—if it returned at all—would be a miracle.

Psychologists brought puzzles, puppets, and painted stories. Speech therapists offered flashcards and blinking screens. Music drifted in from pianos and lullabies. Specialists filled out clipboards and nodded in meetings, discussing rare conditions and possible regressions.

Everyone had a theory, but no one had a breakthrough.

Then, one day, a food-service worker brought in the child's lunch.

Dressed in a white apron, name tag neatly pinned, he entered quietly—as if not to disturb anything too fragile. He placed the tray in front of her with careful hands.

The girl did not respond.

Before leaving, he paused—almost as if remembering something from another time. He picked up the napkin beside her plate and began to fold it. His fingers moved with slow care—deliberate, unhurried. Not neatly. Not perfectly. But purposefully, as if each crease carried meaning.

When he was done, a small paper boat rested on the tray. He tapped it twice, a soft rhythm—like a quiet signal for launch. Then he lifted his eyes to hers, offered a soft nod, a quick wink, and a slight smile before walking out of the room without a word.

The next day, he came again. This time, he folded a rabbit. The day after that, a flower. Each visit brought something new—quiet shapes folded from cloth, carried on the edge of his lunch cart.

He never spoke, never explained. Every gift ended the same way: two soft taps on the tray, a wink, a smile, and the gentle squeak of wheels rolling away.

She still didn't speak, but her eyes followed him now. Her hands began to mimic his folds—clumsy at first, then with more intention. By the fourth day, she watched the door, waiting for the sound of his cart squeaking down the hall.

By the seventh day, she had folded her own napkin creation ready to show him.

And on the fourteenth day, he placed a crane on her tray. She stared at it for a long time. Then, in a fragile voice no one had heard before, she spoke a single word:

"Bird."

She didn't say it to the doctors. Not to the nurses. Not even to her parents. She said it to him.

The room went still. He smiled, nodded again, and left.

The staff was stunned. Urgent consultations were called. Specialists returned with new charts and updated labels.

"What intervention did he use?"

"Was it a known method?"

"Do we have documentation?"

Later, someone questioned him—kindly, yet thoroughly.

"Are you trained in therapeutic techniques?"

"Do you understand child psychology?"

"Was this some form of nonverbal communication therapy?"

The food-service worker shook his head. "I *used to fold paper for my daughter when storms scared her,"* he said.

They logged the event, adjusted her diagnosis, and added foot-notes.

The specialists used words like *"breakthrough," "response trigger,"* and *"emotional access point."* But no report could explain the reason she had spoken—or the way she hummed now and then while folding napkins of her own—or how she now greeted others with the same small wink and smile she had learned from him.

He kept delivering her lunch. He kept folding napkins. A fox. A star. A heart.

Sometimes she folded one back and left it on his cart. Sometimes they traded shapes—small gestures with unspoken meanings, like a quiet language only the two of them understood.

She spoke a little more—slowly and sparingly. A word here. A sentence there. Often quiet, but unmistakably her own.

The doctors adjusted their expectations. The therapists added new terms to their charts. But the girl never asked for their acknowledgment. The food-service worker never sought their approval. He simply returned each day, folded something fragile, and offered it without fanfare.

One day, he wasn't on the schedule. She watched the hallway door, waiting for the familiar wheels and gentle steps. Instead, another worker appeared with her tray.

She didn't speak that day. Or the next.

On the third day, when he finally stepped into her room with a tray in hand and a gentle smile, she looked up—eyes wide.

"I *missed you!*" she said softly, the words breaking into a smile.

The napkin that day was a butterfly.

In a hospital filled with those trained to heal, it was one unseen, unassuming worker—with nothing but a cloth square and a quiet presence—who was the first to make a difference.

THE JUNK DRAWER

Most of us have a drawer somewhere that we avoid opening. It's where we stash the odds and ends we don't know what to do with—things that once mattered, might matter again, or feel too personal to throw away. It's messy, private, and strangely comforting to ignore. But what if that drawer isn't just in your kitchen? What if we all carry an inner junk drawer—filled with memories, regrets, and pieces of ourselves we're not ready to face? And what if someone noticed—not to judge or fix—but to gently help us sort through what still matters... and what we can finally let go of?

He won't brush aside the bruised and the hurt and he won't disregard the small and insignificant, but he'll steadily and firmly set things right.

- Isaiah 42:3 (MSG)

The storm came in fast.

It announced itself suddenly—low gray light, sheets of rain sweeping sideways, a crack of thunder that rattled the window-panes.

Inside the small house, she sat curled up on the couch beneath a frayed throw blanket, her feet tucked under her, a half-finished cup of tea cooling on the table. She had planned to let the storm pass in silence, to keep her thoughts safely locked behind the noise of rain.

That's when she saw him.

A figure beneath the tree outside her window—standing still. No umbrella. No coat. His posture was calm, his hands at his sides, as though the storm had nothing to do with him.

She drew the curtain back just enough to see better. He wasn't pacing or searching for shelter. He wasn't speaking to anyone. Just still.

A part of her wanted to ignore him. She had learned to look away from things that might draw her in. But she couldn't.

She went to the front door and cracked it open. Her voice came out hesitant, careful. *"Are you all right?"*

He lifted his head. Through the downpour, his eyes met hers—calm and steady. Not desperate, like she expected. There was even a trace of warmth in his expression as he stepped toward her porch, unhurried and strangely untouched by the rain.

"Storms don't bother me."

The faint smile that followed made her shoulders loosen before she realized it.

Something in her wanted to shut the door again. She didn't invite people in anymore—hadn't for a long time. Yet, without thinking, she opened the door wider. *"You can come in if you need to wait it out."*

He paused at the threshold, as if letting her change her mind. She didn't. He nodded and stepped inside.

"Tea?" Her voice came too quickly. She didn't wait for an answer—already heading to the kitchen, grateful for the excuse to keep her hands busy.

"Yes, thank you," he said, and somehow it felt as though he were the one doing her a kindness.

He sat down at the kitchen table like someone used to quiet rooms, his presence filling the space without pressing against it.

"Nice kitchen," he said, his eyes traveling gently over the room.

She shrugged. *"It's small. But I try to keep it in order."*

He nodded once. His gaze lingered briefly on the fridge, where a strawberry-shaped magnet held a yellowed recipe card—her grandmother's handwriting, her grandmother's pie. She hadn't baked it in years. He didn't comment, just noticed. Somehow that felt kind.

Then his eyes shifted—not with intrusion but with a quiet knowing—to the drawer beneath the counter. The one that stuck when you pulled it. The one she always kept shut.

Her breath hitched for a moment.

"That one's a mess," she said, attempting a laugh that faltered

halfway. *"Just my junk drawer."*

His expression didn't change—no judgment, no surprise. *"Everyone has one,"* he said.

The words settled between them. He didn't add anything else.

"I've been meaning to clean it out," she added, her arms folding tighter across her chest. The sharp edge in her tone surprised even her.

He didn't respond. The silence wasn't strained; it felt natural, as if words weren't needed yet.

Her eyes shifted to the drawer again. She knew what lay inside. Not just clutter. Fragments she had kept instead of facing. Reminders of things she had buried rather than confront.

For years she had lived as though closing the drawer was the same as letting go.

Without knowing why, she crossed the room and placed her hand on the handle.

It stuck—just as it always did—before giving way with a soft groan.

Inside was a small, chaotic world of rubber bands, pens that no longer worked, crumpled receipts, chargers for devices long gone, a bent paperclip, a shopping list scrawled in haste: *bread, bananas, hope.*

Her fingers brushed deeper, finding the very things she'd tried hardest not to find.

A faded photograph, edges curled.

A birthday card with handwriting that trembled across the page.

A hospital bracelet, still holding the imprint of a night she had tried to forget.

A sealed envelope she had never sent.

She gripped the pieces as if holding them could keep them from being seen.

"It's just junk," she whispered, the words almost breaking as they left her mouth.

He rose from his chair, tea still in hand, and stopped a few steps away.

"May I?" he asked softly, like someone asking permission to step onto holy ground.

Her instinct was to refuse. Close the drawer. Pretend again.

But she nodded.

He moved closer, unhurried, carrying no hint of judgment.

He reached first for the photo, holding it as if it were fragile glass.

"You haven't stopped loving her," he said—not as an accusation, but as something true that deserved to be spoken aloud.

Next came the card. He traced the edge with his thumb.

"This still matters." He spoke with reverence, as if honoring a memory that still breathed.

His hand touched the bracelet.

"You weren't alone that night." His words landed gently, refusing to press further.

Last was the envelope. "

This one's still waiting to be said." It didn't sound like a command. More like an invitation that had been there all along.

Tears slipped down her cheeks—quiet, un-dramatic—the grief of someone who had finally run out of places to hide.

He said nothing more. Didn't explain. Didn't pry. He simply held each item as if it had always belonged in his hands.

To him they weren't junk or clutter at all—only pieces, prayers, wounds, and the fragments of wishful thinking.

"Why does any of this matter to you?" Her voice barely rose above the clock's slow ticking.

He met her gaze—steady, unflinching. *"Because nothing is wasted in my hands."*

Then, one by one, he returned the pieces to her—the photo, the card, the bracelet, the letter—placing each with the same devotion he had shown in holding them.

She glanced at the drawer. It hadn't been emptied, but it felt different. Lighter. As though the weight had shifted simply because it had been seen.

Outside, the storm softened to a hush, rain traced the windows like a slow, wandering fingertip.

Her eyes went to the table—her cup of tea still warm, the chair still waiting where he had sat. She wasn't ready to let him go. *"You're welcome to finish your tea,"* she said quietly, as if afraid even the sound of her own voice might break the moment.

"*Thank you*," he replied, returning to the chair with a gentleness that felt like presence, not intrusion.

His eyes settled again on the items still clutched in her hands. "*I'd like to hear more about these.*"

She looked down at them, then up at him. For reasons she couldn't explain, she felt completely safe.

She sat across from him and laid the items out again on the table, her fingers lingering, as if reluctant to let each piece go.

For the first time in years, she was ready to tell her story.

THE YESSES

There's a strange pressure to say yes to everything—every opportunity, invitation, or open door—especially when we're afraid of missing out or falling behind. But not every yes leads to life. Sometimes, the fear of missing out causes us to miss what matters most. And in the rush to keep all our options open, we can end up closed off to the one thing that was meant to shape everything else.

One handful of peaceful repose is better than two fistfuls of worried work—more spitting into the wind.

- Ecclesiastes 4:6 (MSG)

The first invitation arrived on a Monday morning.

A small group of friends was entering a 48-hour film competition—write, shoot, and edit a short film in one weekend. They asked if he would join them.

"We need your voice—your heart, your depth. We're building the entire story around trust and truth."

It wasn't glamorous, but it felt right. These friends knew him. Not the résumé version, not the curated profile, but the real him. The one who carried both scars and stories. It was the type of project that wouldn't make him famous but might use his skills for a greater good.

He said *yes.*

Then, on Wednesday, another opportunity surfaced: a weekend retreat hosted by a startup incubator with big names, big ideas, and big potential.

He'd been to one before and remembered how the talk about *"vision"* often slid into ego, how easily ambition turned into competition.

But what if this was the door he'd been waiting for—the one that could launch everything? What if he let it slip by?

He said another *yes.*

By Thursday afternoon, a message came from a content creator he followed—someone with a massive online following.

"We're filming a weekend co-lab! Come shoot reels, vlogs, behind-the-scenes clips—build your brand and be seen."

The idea was tempting. A chance to be noticed. To grow his

platform. He knew the content they made—not necessarily bad, just not what he was about. The jokes, the energy, the edge. He'd have to fake confidence, maybe even compromise a little. But the views, the exposure, the potential. He didn't want to be left behind.

Yes again.

Later that night, a cousin texted him about a weekend at a beach house—old friends, spontaneous fun, and maybe a little extra...

...whatever that meant.

He knew what that crowd was like. He'd grown past it. The partying. The emptiness. The pressure to pretend he was fine with things he no longer found fun or fulfilling. But still... part of him didn't want to look self-righteous. And honestly, part of him missed the simplicity of not having to care. After all, what could it hurt?

He said *yes*, even to that.

By Friday morning, his phone wouldn't stop buzzing—four group chats competing for his attention.

The film team had already written the first few scenes.
The startup group was finalizing schedules and pitch decks.
The content creator sent a shot list and a meet-up time.
The beach gang was already posting photos of themselves having drinks by the pool.

He kept bouncing between threads, trying to sound present in each one.

That night, he showed up late to the film team's first shoot. The energy had shifted. They were polite, but focused. The story had developed without him. The part he was supposed to lead had been rewritten. He provided feedback, attempted to jump in, but left early to attend the startup mixer.

By the time he arrived at the mixer, the session was wrapping up. He stood awkwardly by the snack table, hovering near conversations he wasn't part of.

The next morning, he met the co-lab crew. Lights. Cameras. Influencers everywhere. He smiled, posed, and did a few takes. But none of it felt real. He wasn't himself anymore—just a version carefully crafted for likes.

He left early again and drove to the beach.

They greeted him with cheers, but the sun was already fading, and most people were checked out or passed out. He stayed the night. Not because it was fun—just because going home felt heavier.

By Sunday night, everything had ended.

The film had been submitted—his name missing from the credits.
The retreat had wrapped up. He'd missed the pitch window.
The videos had gone live. He was barely in the footage.
The beach trip? Just a haze of noise and small talk.

Four yeses. Four promises. Four compromises.

He sat on his bed that night, scrolling through highlight reels of the weekend. Faces lit by filters. Stories accompanied by soundtracks. Snapshots of joy he hadn't felt.

And he thought about the first invitation—the only one that had lined up with who he was—the only one where he was wanted for the right reasons. The only one that had made something in his soul sit still in a good way.

He had said *yes*. Then *yes* again. And again. And again—until the others buried the first.

And the *yes* that mattered most...

... had been emptied of its meaning.

THE FLASHLIGHT

Most of us prefer to stay where it feels safe—places where things are already good, where we don't have to stand out, and where there's little risk of being misunderstood. But the light that truly makes a difference isn't meant for the easy spaces. It's meant for the dark—for moments, people, and places where hope feels far away. What if we stopped trying to fit in and started letting our light shine where it's actually needed?

The light shines in the darkness, and the darkness has not overcome it.

-1 John 1:5 (NIV)

He carried it everywhere—a flashlight, silver and sleek, always on.

Even in broad daylight he held it out in front of him, thumb pressed to the switch, convinced the beam was there—though the sun swallowed it whole. He couldn't see the light, but he knew it was there. And that gave him a strange sense of comfort.

He walked sidewalks, wandered parks, passed through markets and plazas—always pointing the light forward. But no one seemed to notice. People glanced past him, through him—rarely at him, never at the flashlight.

A few gave puzzled glances. Some smirked. One child, squinting into the sun, tugged on her mother's skirt.

"Why's he carrying a flashlight in the sunshine?"

"Shh," the mother whispered, giving the man a quick, apologetic smile before pulling the girl away.

He tried not to let it bother him, but deep down... it did.

"This light matters," he said under his breath, jaw clenched against a familiar ache. "It matters."

But the longer he carried it, the more invisible it seemed. Still, he couldn't bring himself to switch it off.

He remembered the dark. Not just the absence of light—but the creeping kind. The kind that seeps into your thoughts and settles in your bones. He remembered feeling lost, afraid, and alone.

So every evening, before the sun dipped too low, he hurried home. He never stayed out past dusk. He couldn't risk it. Even with the flashlight, the dark still terrified him. Better to be home. Better to be safe. Better to never find out if the light really worked.

Then came the evening when everything went wrong. The day lingered longer than usual, and he'd wandered farther than he realized. By the time he noticed the golden sky stretching across the rooftops, it was too late. He was still blocks from home. And the sun was sinking fast.

Panic sparked in his chest. He quickened his pace, his hand gripping the flashlight tighter.

That's when he passed the stranger—standing on a corner near a bench. Older. Calm. A presence that seemed to quiet the noise around him.

"*Your flashlight,*" the stranger said—curious, not unkind. "*Why do you keep it on during the day?*"

He froze. The question wasn't new to him, but the voice carried no hint of mockery—only genuine interest.

"*I don't like the dark,*" he admitted softly, eyes lowered to the ground. "*I'm afraid of the dark.*"

The stranger tilted his head slightly, as if weighing the answer.

"*Then maybe you don't know what it was made to do.*"

"*What do you mean?*" he asked, frowning as he shifted the flashlight in his grip.

"*You've been trying to prove it works in the daylight.*" The stranger gave a soft laugh. "*But flashlights don't shine in the sun... because they were never meant to.*"

He glanced down at the flashlight. The beam was still on—just faint, barely visible in the golden hour.

"*It's not designed for the daylight,*" the stranger went on, his voice warm but steady. "*It's meant to be seen in the dark. That's when it changes things. That's when it matters.*"

As they spoke, the sun sank behind the hills. Shadows crept across the streets, climbed the walls, pooled at their feet. The warmth slipped from the air.

And for the man with the flashlight, fear rose again.

The darkness had come.

But then the beam appeared—bright, pure, undeniable. For the first time, the light in his hand could truly be seen.

Others nearby noticed too. People who had passed him earlier now slowed. Their eyes followed the beam—not the man. A few even began walking beside him, quietly falling in step.

And in that moment, the fear that had gripped him for years began to slip away.

His flashlight wasn't strange anymore. It was seen. It was needed. And wherever he pointed it, the darkness gave way.

He had misunderstood the benefit of his light. It wasn't proof of his preparedness. It wasn't a performance to earn applause in the light.

It was a guide for when the darkness came—never if... always when.

He looked down at the flashlight in his hand. Still steady. Still on. But now—it made a difference.

He kept walking. Not to escape the dark—but to move into it.

Each step felt different now. Purposeful. Free.

He slowed when he noticed someone stumbling at the edge of the path. Without hesitation, he turned the beam toward them.

The person looked up, startled at first—then their face softened in the glow.

He smiled back—not out of pride or relief, but because he finally understood the reason for his light.

Not to prove anything in daylight, but to shine where the darkness runs deepest.

THE SELF-AWARENESS WEEKEND

We live in an age when the search for self has become its own religion. Where honesty is often rehearsed, and healing is measured in outward signs. We've learned to speak the language of growth, to name our wounds, and to display progress like a badge—visible, polished, incomplete. But beneath the surface of sincerity, many still feel unseen, unhealed, and unsure if we're truly becoming whole—or simply mastering the art of disguise. What if the transformation we seek is not transformation at all, but another performance in a world that rewards appearance over truth?

Everyone's after the dishonest dollar, little people and big people alike. Prophets and priests and everyone in between twist words and doctor truth. My people are broken—shattered!—and they put on Band-Aids, saying, "It's not so bad. You'll be just fine. **"But things are not "just fine!."**

- Jeremiah 6:13,14 (MSG)

It sold out in less than an hour.

The Deep Work Weekend: Becoming Fully You.

Tickets came with a bamboo-bound journal, a curated mindfulness playlist, and an embossed name tag printed in a font called *Organic Bold*. Guests could choose from Basic Entry, Premium Circle Access, or VIP Authenticity Coaching with the keynote speaker—a former monk turned brand strategist.

The promotional video opened with slow-motion shots of glowing people laughing barefoot in a forest. A soft-spoken celebrity voice-over promised, *"You're not broken. You're becoming."*

A popular reviewer called it *"like therapy, but with better lighting."* Another wrote, *"It's where I finally learned to speak my truth—and gain a following."*

Everyone was there—Influencers, life coaches, burned-out creatives with imposter syndrome, a few church leaders *"just to observe,"* a barista who got in on a scholarship, and a couple of authors who promised not to promote their latest books—though they eventually did.

The retreat center looked the part: reclaimed-wood walls, polished-concrete floors, succulents tucked into handcrafted clay pots, and string lights overhead that resembled stars if you squinted. Even the bathrooms had affirmation cards propped on the sinks:

"YOU ARE ENOUGH."
"LET YOUR SOUL BLOOM."
"IMAGINE THE NEW YOU!"

That first night, they gathered in a wide circle. A whiteboard near the door declared in thick green marker: "LEAVE YOUR

MASKS AT THE DOOR." Right beside it stood a ring-light and a phone-charging station.

The facilitator wore loose linen pants and a hand-woven scarf. He held a ceramic mug that read, "Be YOU—Do YOU." He opened the evening with a grounding exercise, speaking low and slow.

"Feel your body... now ask it what it needs."

His tone dripped with gentle authority. People nodded solemnly, breathing in deep, slow exhales.

Following the exercise, participants were told to open the custom retreat app on their phones to add notes. They moved on to vision boards, then to a guided-forgiveness ritual—optional but *"highly encouraged."* Later, they sat cross-legged on meditation cushions, journaling through prompts like:

"What area of my life requires more recognition?"
"How am I giving away my power?"
"Is my self-care routine Instagram-worthy or merely functional?"

By the second day, it was clear who was *really* doing the work—those crying openly in breakout rooms, offering unsolicited coaching, and peppering conversations with phrases like *"my sacred wound,"* *"inner alignment,"* and *"energetic boundaries."*

Lunch featured small-batch kombucha, wild-rice bowls with jackfruit, fermented beets, and activated seeds. Conversations swirled with lines such as:

"I'm holding space for that."
"That doesn't serve me anymore."
"I'm releasing what no longer aligns with my media strategy."

The weekend was going perfectly according to plan—until Saturday night.

It happened during the *mirror-moment* session, a candle-lit circle for sharing one's most authentic self. A woman—quiet until then—raised her hand without being called on. Her voice trembled.

"I can't do this anymore."

The words barely escaped her lips. The room paused, heads tilting toward her.

"Not just this retreat," she continued, taking a shaky breath. *"This... this performance. I'm tired of pretending I'm okay just because I can name my trauma in a poetic way."*

Silence followed—not the sacred kind, but the kind that feels as if the air has been knocked out of the room.

She went on, her voice raw. *"I don't feel seen. Not here. Not anywhere. And I hate that I even came hoping this would fix that."*

She let out a nervous laugh, cracking halfway through. *"I made a vision board yesterday. You know what was on it? Peace. I just wanted peace."*

For a moment, no one moved. The candles flickered against the silence.

Her voice began to tremble. *"But even here, I feel like I have to be someone. Be healed. Be inspirational. Be enough. What if I'm just... not?"*

A heavy pause. Then, almost on cue, the familiar script resumed.

"Have you tried breath-work?"
"Inner-child journaling helped me a lot."

"*You might want to try a spirit-cleansing.*"

One of the authors in the circle cleared her throat. "*There's a chapter in my new book... it might help...*" Her voice trailed off into the awkward stillness.

Someone reached over with a lavender-scented tissue, their touch quick and practiced.

"*Just remember,*" someone chimed in, quoting an earlier mantra: "'*You... are... enough.*'"

She nodded slowly, but her eyes said otherwise.

No one asked her name. No one followed up.

The facilitator—seasoned in such moments—leaned forward with a polished half-smile. "*Thank you for sharing that,*" he said smoothly. "*Thank you for your bravery. And now—before we wrap—don't forget to tag the retreat handle when you post your reflections.*"

By morning, the hashtags were trending again.

On Sunday afternoon, they gathered one last time in a closing circle. The facilitator invited each person to "*share one truth you discovered this weekend.*"

A man in a wide-brimmed hat spoke first, his voice measured. "*I'm learning to honor my boundaries.*"

A woman wearing four symbolic necklaces—a cross, a moon, a feather, and a star—lowered her eyes and nodded once. "*I deserve softness.*"

Someone else jumped in quickly. "*I've always been too much for people, and I'm okay with that now.*"

Another participant glanced around the group, tilting her head with a small smile. *"I've discovered that I'm actually an empath."*

Polite nods and supportive affirmations made their way around the group circle.

A professional photographer gathered them beneath the canopy of string lights for the closing shot.

"Now give me raw."—click, click.

"Now grounded."—click, click.

"Now show me some joy."—click, click.

They shifted poses—some laughing, some serious. Filtered, but candid—candid, but curated.

Click, click—*"Done."*

They asked the photographer to share the photos. Once they confirmed receipt on their phones, they drifted away—each to their own bungalow.

By dinner, twenty-seven posts had gone up, each one ending with the same closing line:

"Look out, world, this weekend changed my life!"

No one noticed that the woman who had broken down the night before wasn't in any of the pictures.

In fact, she hadn't shown up that morning.

THE BAKER'S LOAF

Our world is obsessed with scale—everything must be faster, bigger, and instantly accessible. But not everything is meant to be duplicated. When we try to systematize what was meant to be intimate, we lose its essence. What if the very things we're trying to reproduce were only ever meant to grow through the slow, sacred work of relationship?

Go stand at the crossroads and look around. Ask for directions to the old road, the tried-and-true road. Then take it. Discover the right route for your souls. But they said, "Nothing doing. We aren't going that way."

- Jeremiah 6:16 (MSG)

He never wrote down a single recipe.

Years of early mornings and quiet prayers whispered over rising dough shaped his technique.

He didn't bake for business. He baked for beauty—though he would never have called it that.

He shaped each loaf by memory and touch, measuring not by weight but by feel—pinches of salt, handfuls of flour, water warmed only to the point his fingers approved. Every motion carried the quiet certainty of someone who trusted his hands more than the scales.

Each freshly baked loaf had its own distinct character—a crispy golden crust split in unique ways, showing off airy insides. Yet, they all shared a faint, yeasty scent; an enchanting element missing in brand-factory-made bread.

People said it tasted like comfort, like childhood, like the smell of home when someone who loves you is cooking just for you.

However, he was much more than just a baker.

He remembered birthdays with no need of a calendar. He knew who preferred crusty ends and who liked theirs warm, soft, and torn straight from the middle. Children would sneak in before school for the smell alone and leave with a complimentary crusty heel wrapped in wax paper.

The people didn't just love his bread. They loved *him*.

And he baked as if it were a sacred act. As if every loaf carried not only flour and yeast, but memory and joy.

An elderly widow came each morning, sitting in the same seat, hands wrapped around a roll she barely touched. The baker always brought her tea before she asked.

A young couple, still learning how to be married, would walk to the shop on Saturdays, split a loaf down the center, and talk about their plans for the future, smiling over hot chocolates he set before them.

A delivery boy—who never had enough money—would always leave with something warm in his hands and a dusting of flour on his shirt.

The bread became part of their lives. Not just something they would always remember, but something that remembered them.

One bustling Saturday morning, a man in a tailored suit stepped into the bakery.

He wore shiny shoes and used words like *"expansion," "branding,"* and *"nationwide distribution."*

"This bread too delicious for one location," he said, running a manicured hand along the counter. *"Your bread could reach hundreds of thousands... maybe more, if we do it right."*

The baker stayed silent, listening with curiosity and a trace of skepticism.

The man leaned in, his smile easy. *"You give us your recipe... we'll take care of the rest."* His voice had a smoothness born of experience, the kind that put people at ease. *"We'll provide the facilities, measure everything—flour to the gram, yeast by volume, temperature by algorithm. You won't have to lift a finger. And of course, your name goes on the label."*

The baker didn't answer immediately. It sounded like a gift. It also sounded like a trap.

He wondered: *Would the bread still remember people if it no longer came from his hands? Could something produced in bulk still carry love in its crust? Would his name mean more—or less—when printed on a package?*

He looked down at his hands, calloused, yet soft with flour. He really didn't want more.

When word of the man's offer reached the town, many told the baker he'd be foolish not to expand.

He still hesitated—not because he didn't care, but because he cared too much. He wanted more people to taste the warmth, to feel the connection his bread carried. And just as deeply, he wanted to know the people who would eat it.

But the businessman refused to take no for an answer.

"Look," he said, placing a hand over his heart with exaggerated sincerity, "*I know this isn't just bread to you. I can see that. But think of it this way—what if your gift was never meant to stay in this small shop? What if all these years of kneading and shaping and praying over dough were just the beginning? What if this bread—your bread—was meant to feed not just a town, but a generation?*"

He lowered his voice as if revealing a sacred truth. "*You could be a name people remember... a comfort in kitchens far from here.*"

The baker wanted to say no. But the vision the man painted was too grand, too flattering, too full of purpose to ignore.

Maybe this is how I can touch more lives, the baker thought.

So, he hesitantly agreed.

It didn't take long for the wheels to start spinning.

The baker tried to reduce his life's passion to a series of steps, but love, once packaged, becomes formulaic.

The crusts lost their essence; the bread still rose—but not in spirit.

Ovens were automated, assembly lines were built, workers timed the kneading, and preservatives were added to extend shelf life. Plastic bags were printed and branded with the baker's image, and loaves were shipped in bulk crates to supermarkets everywhere.

His bread—once warm and personal—now sat on store shelves beside generic breads, buns, and muffins, just another shopping option, far from what had once made it special.

No one smelled it in the morning. No one closed their eyes after the first bite. No one felt like it was baked just for them.

The business grew. Billboards went up, commercials aired, the stock rose—and the brand became a household name.

But the baker—the one with the hands that remembered—was no longer part of it. He watched from afar as his name spread wider than his reach ever had, but he felt smaller with every mile it traveled.

Long gone were the people who used to drive from neighboring towns just to stand in his tiny shop and take photos of the golden crusts stacked behind fogged glass.

The bakery still stood—but it had become a relic. An old photograph hung in the hallway of a corporate office.

But one early morning, he unlocked its door again.
Just to remember.

The wooden counters were worn smooth, but familiar. The silence felt like an old friend.

He tied on his apron and measured the flour by hand—slowly, with reverence. A pinch of salt, a pour of water warmed to just the right degree. The dough clung to his fingers, alive again, as the yeasty aroma began to fill the room.

He baked only one loaf.

As he pulled it from the oven, the bell over the front door rang.

A young man lingered in the doorway, hesitant yet drawn in by the aroma.

He didn't speak or point or ask for a menu. He simply stood there, as if the smell of bread had awakened something in him he hadn't known was missing.

The baker studied him—the coat too thin for the season, the eyes shadowed with fatigue, a kind of hunger that went deeper than the stomach.

In that quiet moment, the baker understood: his work had never been about scale or brand or growth. It was about people—about this man, right here.

So he offered the loaf, not for payment, but freely, as if returning it to the purpose for which it had been baked all along.

The young man accepted it, holding it with both hands as if it were something alive—something sacred.

The baker smiled with a deep sense of satisfaction—a feeling he hadn't experienced in a long time.

This smile was unlike the one stamped on plastic bags in the supermarkets. It was the smile of someone who had recovered his purpose—and remembered the sacred potential baked into a single hand-shaped loaf of bread.

THE VIEW FROM THE TOP

Some chase success so fiercely they forget to bring anyone with them. When people become means to an end, and connection is measured by usefulness, the climb may be fast—but it's also lonely. What looks like progress can quietly shape a lie, until the view from the top reveals just how much was lost along the way.

Don't push your way to the front; don't sweet-talk your way to the top. Put yourself aside, and help others get ahead. Don't be obsessed with getting your own advantage. Forget yourselves long enough to lend a helping hand.

Philippians 2:3,4 (MSG)

He was always moving.

He moved from one job to the next, one friend group to another, one conversation to the next—dropping names as he went.

People liked him... at first. He had a charm that fit every room. He listened just enough. He laughed at the right time. He made you feel seen—until he didn't need to see you anymore.

He kept things light. Never too deep. Never too long. Deep meant messy, and messy slowed you down.

He wasn't cruel—just relentless. Not for birthdays. Not for breakups. Not for anyone who couldn't offer him another rung on the ladder.

He never said it out loud, but his motto was clear: keep climbing—no matter the cost.

He told himself it wasn't selfish. It was focused. Discipline was what separated the successful from the sentimental.

He remembered the night his college roommate asked him to skip a networking dinner to celebrate a small music gig. "I can't," he'd said, buttoning his blazer. "*Opportunities don't wait.*" The band broke up a year later, but the contact he made that night got him his first real job.

He told himself that missing his father's retirement party wasn't personal—just timing. "*If I want to provide for my family someday, I have to say yes to the client first.*"

He believed late-night emails were a sign of dedication. That cutting emotions out of decisions made him strong. That hard choices proved he was built for leadership.

He called himself a networker, an influencer, a leader. But in reality, he was a collector—of people, moments, and borrowed influence.

At first, no one noticed. He said all the right things. Posted all the right quotes. Preached all the right values. And made you feel lucky to be included.

But there was a pattern.

He borrowed ideas without credit. He told stories that weren't his to tell. He promised help and disappeared. He invited people close—but only when he needed something.

A mentor once cautioned him. *"You're climbing too fast to notice who you're leaving behind."*

He laughed it off. *"I'm just focused,"* he said. Then he changed the subject and quietly dropped the mentor.

One by one, those who had once admired him retreated. Not out of anger. Just wisdom.

He replaced them quickly. New names. Fresh faces. Different circles. Because ambition doesn't rest, and it certainly doesn't look back.

Eventually, he reached what looked like the top. Big influencer. Big following. Big view.

He had the job he wanted, the accolades, and the seat at the table. But the air was thin, and the space was quiet. After all, no one stays near a ladder once they've been stepped on.

He tried to host a celebration. Sent the invites, booked the venue, and wrote a heartfelt post.

Few came. Most declined. Some didn't answer at all.

He stood there, drink in hand, in a room full of strangers who all wanted something from him—a connection, a favor, a chance to do what he had done.

He smiled. He made small talk. But their eyes didn't really see him.

And for the first time, he wondered, *Did I climb my way here—or use people as stairs?*

The question echoed in his mind, but no one answered.

The summit couldn't give him what he'd been reaching for all along. You can climb to the top and still be completely alone.

Real love doesn't grow up there—it grows in the pauses. In being there for others, even when it's inconvenient. In choosing to stay, when there's nothing to gain.

And he had skipped all of that.

Later that night, he scrolled through old messages. Names he hadn't texted in years. Moments he once called friendship—but now realized had been trades.

He thought about sending a message. But didn't know what to say. Because when you've lived on the surface, going deep feels like drowning.

And yet, somewhere in the quiet, something stirred: a silent revelation.

Maybe he had climbed in the wrong direction.

Maybe the real ascent was not upward—but downward.

Downward into apology.
Downward into presence.

Downward into healing.

Maybe it was time to return—not to the summit, but to the people he'd hurried past. The ones who once believed he could become more—more than image, more than hustle, closer to who he really was.

Perhaps the view he'd been searching for was never at the top at all...

... but at eye level, in the faces of those he'd left behind.

THE CENTER TABLE

Many people believe that truth and love are on opposite sides of the table—that you can either say what's real or show someone grace, but not both. And most of us, if we're honest, lean one way or the other. But what if truth and love are inseparable?

The Word became flesh and made his dwelling among us. We have seen his glory, the glory of the one and only Son, who came from the Father, full of grace and truth.

- John 1:14 (NIV)

It was the kind of café where no one rushed you. Mismatched chairs, chipped mugs, and a chalkboard menu that smudged when it rained. There was always just enough noise to feel—and just enough quiet to think.

Behind the counter hung two hand-painted signs.

One read: **ALWAYS SPEAK THE TRUTH.**

The other: **ALWAYS SHOW LOVE.**

No one remembered exactly when the signs first went up. They'd been there as long as anyone could recall.

The owner—a quiet, steady man with more wrinkles than words—never explained them. When asked, he'd only shrug and say with a quiet warmth, 'Both matter.'"Both matter."

But over time, the signs shaped the room.

Some regulars took to the first sign as a motto.

"*In here, we speak the truth—whether you like it or not,*" they'd say, especially when correcting someone, challenging an opinion, or calling out a behavior they believed crossed the line.

They prided themselves on honesty, even when it stung. They sat by the window mostly, where the light was sharp and nothing could hide.

Others leaned toward the second sign.

"*The world's hard enough already—what people need is kindness and understanding,*" they'd say, offering reassuring smiles as they spoke.

Without a word, they were the first to cover someone's bill or refill an empty cup. They liked to sit together in the back corner, where the light was soft and the seats were close.

Eventually, the distance between the groups became more than just a difference of opinion. It became a boundary not to be crossed.

Some started avoiding certain tables altogether. A few customers quietly disappeared.

Even the barista noticed it—how the air in the café felt thinner when the two groups were in the room at the same time.

They didn't argue loudly. They didn't have to. The silence between them carried more weight than shouting ever could. Every glance, every tightened jaw, every unspoken word was etched clearly on their faces—like a conversation no one else could hear, but everyone could see.

One Tuesday afternoon, a young woman walked in. She looked a little unsure at first—pausing just inside the door, like someone entering the middle of a conversation already in progress. She ordered tea and sat at a table in the center of the room. The one equidistant from both groups.

No one thought much of it—at first.

But she came back the next day. Then the next. And the next... always at the same center table.

She didn't belong to either group, or she didn't try to. Her voice was quiet, but the questions she asked made people think.

And when she spoke the truth, it didn't come with a blade. When she showed love, it didn't come with an apology.

Some tried to claim her.

A man from the front tables leaned over one day. "*I like how you're not afraid to be honest. Too many people sugarcoat everything.*"

She smiled but didn't reply.

Later that week, someone from the back corner offered, "*It's good to see someone choose love over intolerance.*"

Again, just a smile. No agreement, no correction.

And that's when the questions started.

"*Who does she think she is?*"
"*Why won't she pick a side?*"
"*She's afraid to take a stand.*"

"*If she's trying to connect with all of us, she won't connect with any of us.*"

But she didn't seem to care about the skeptical comments or the suspicious looks.

One morning, someone stormed out of the café, accusing others of being too narrow-minded. She noticed they had left a scarf behind. Slipping it over her arm, she stepped outside, crossed the street, caught up with them, and offered it back with quiet gentleness.

When she returned, a man lingered by the door—his coat thin, his hands chapped, his eyes scanning for a place to belong. The air around him carried the faint, sour scent of the street: sweat, rain, and survival. His beard was patchy, his shoulders drawn tight against the cold.

She held the door open a little longer than necessary.

"*Would you like to sit with me?*"

She didn't preach. She didn't explain herself.She just kept show-ing up—center table, every time.

And slowly, without meaning to, people sat near her. Not many at first. Just a few who were tired of the arguing. Tired of having to choose between being heard and being held.

They didn't always agree with her. But they felt safe.

One morning, after the rush had passed, the barista and the owner stood at the counter drying mugs, side by side.

She leaned toward him. "*Do you think she understands the signs?*"

The owner looked over at the center table. She was laughing with someone from the back and someone from the front—both leaning in, both listening.

A quiet smile crossed his face, as though he carried a secret only he knew.

"*I think she is the sign.*"

THE WILDFLOWERS

Many things lose their wonder when too tightly controlled. We try to box in what's beautiful, polish what's wild, and protect what should remain unfenced. But what if the truest kind of beauty was never meant to be cultivated or contained at all? What if it grows best in the unexpected places, far from the systems we've built to contain it?

"A farmer planted seed... some fell on the road... some fell in the gravel... some fell in the weeds... some fell on the good earth, and produced a harvest beyond his wildest dreams."

- (Jesus) Matthew 13:3-9 abbr. (MSG)

He always loved beauty.

Even as a boy, he'd stop to admire the curve of a leaf or the way sunlight spilled through branches like melted gold. So, when he grew older, gardening became more than a hobby—it became his language, his way of arranging the world into something he could trust.

He chose a small plot of land just outside of town, far enough to feel quiet, close enough to be admired.

He began to plant.

He worked the soil until every clump broke smooth between his fingers, unwilling to leave a single stone out of place. The rows he measured were ruler-straight, each one checked and rechecked until it lined up with the next. When he planted the seeds, he set them at precise depths, pressing the earth over them as if sealing a promise—determined that nothing be left to chance.

And he built a wooden fence around the edges—to protect what was delicate from what was wild.

Every morning, he walked the paths with his hands behind his back and a quiet smile on his face.

Here was his sanctuary.

The roses lined the walkway like royalty in procession, their blooms lifted high as though aware of their own beauty. Nearby, the herbs spilled their fragrance into the air, a soft reminder of his patient tending. Flowering bushes grew strong and full, each one nestled in its assigned bed like a child tucked beneath a blanket. As he stood back to take it all in, a quiet pride rose in him—everything in its place, everything as he had intended.

Visitors came often, always marveling at the order, the symmetry, and the comforting knowledge that beauty could be arranged.

The gardener couldn't hide the pride he felt in his garden. He had done well.

One day, while pruning a vine near the edge of the fence, he saw an old woman standing outside. Her clothes were patched and dusty, and her skin bore the marks of sun and time. But her face held a kind of familiarity—like a favorite song you haven't heard in a long while—joyful and reassuring.

He watched in disbelief as she scattered handfuls of seeds into the open wind, her movements loose and unhurried.

"What are you doing?" he asked, his voice caught between curiosity and caution.

"Sowing," she replied with a careless toss, the breeze catching the seeds as if claiming them for itself. "The wind knows where they belong."

His jaw tightened, his face carrying the weight of disapproval. "But that's not how it works," he protested. "Seeds need care, protection, structure. Out there, they'll never survive."

She only smiled, her eyes bright with a knowing he couldn't grasp, then turned and walked away—her bag empty, her footprints light against the dusty road—leaving him standing amid his perfect rows, his frustration rooted deeper than the soil.

Time slipped by as the seasons turned—spring's first blossoms giving way to summer's fullness, then autumn's fading gold, and finally the stillness of winter. Through it all, the gardener's plot continued to flourish, each row as orderly and vibrant as ever.

Yet he began to notice a change.

Fewer visitors came.

Those who did still admired the beauty, but their wonder no longer lingered.

Some paused only at the gate, offering polite smiles before moving on.

Others asked if they might take a flower or a handful of seeds home. But when he explained the garden was not for picking, they only nodded. Then they left—quietly, as they had come.

One morning, as he walked the fence line that bordered the road, something unexpected caught his eye and stopped him in his tracks. On the edge of the cracked asphalt, just beyond a rusted signpost, a broad swath of wildflowers moved as one in the morning breeze. They weren't arranged in rows or trimmed to size. Their stems bent and swayed with the wind, yet their colors blazed—vibrant, alive, and recklessly beautiful.

He stepped closer, squinting as though to be sure of what he was seeing. They weren't confined to that single patch. They were everywhere—pinks, yellows, deep purples—all blooming where no one had expected them to grow. They spilled from the gaps between stones in the wall, tracing the riverbank with color, climbing behind the schoolhouse, and springing up in the most forgotten corners of town. The sight unsettled him as much as it amazed him. There was a wildness in their beauty that didn't need careful rows or measured hands.

He couldn't decide whether to feel threatened by it—or stand in wonder.

He watched people slow their steps to take in the sight, their faces softening as they paused.

Children bent low, noses nearly brushing the petals, giggling at the sweetness they discovered.

A few gathered small bouquets, clutching them like treasures to carry home.

There was no gate to open, no path to follow, no instructions to read—only beauty spilling freely into every open space: unexpected, uninvited, yet utterly undeniable.

And then he saw the old woman again. She was kneeling beside a cluster of tangled yellow blooms, her hands covered with soil. Her smile reached through every line on her face.

He stepped closer, his voice low with wonder. "*I thought your seeds would never survive.*"

She looked up, unsurprised. "*Many didn't.*" Her gaze swept over the vibrant colors before them. "*But those that did became something no garden could ever hold.*"

"*But there's no control...*" The words came haltingly, caught between frustration and awe. "*There was no guarantee.*"

"*No control on my part,*" she replied, lifting her eyes to the sky. "*The wind knows better than I where the seeds should grow.*"

He stood in silence, watching the breeze stir the petals like dancers in a song only they could hear. Something deep inside him moved—a quiet sense of wonder that no amount of order or design had ever satisfied.

That evening, he returned to his garden. He walked the familiar paths, let his gaze linger on the symmetry, and drew in the fragrance of his safe, enclosed beauty. Then, for the first time in years, he pushed the gate—wide.

And the next morning, with a small pouch of seeds in one hand and his heart in the other, he stepped beyond the fence. He lifted his hand to the wind—and let it decide where beauty would bloom next.

THE THREE CANDLE BEARERS

There are voices that fill rooms for a season—loud, admired, impossible to ignore—until one day they're gone, leaving only an echo. Others strive to leave their mark, pouring themselves into endless effort, yet their work crumbles as soon as the hands stop moving. And then there are quieter voices, the kind that shape hearts in unseen ways. You don't notice their influence at first... until you realize it's still with you long after the noise has faded.

"You didn't choose me, remember; I chose you, and put you in the world to bear fruit, fruit that won't spoil. As fruit bearers, whatever you ask the Father in relation to me, he gives you."

-(Jesus) John 15:16 (MSG)

Darkness came suddenly.

One moment, the world was alive with light—streetlamps humming, windows aglow, the blue shimmer of a thousand screens.

An uneasy hush settled over the city. Power lines hung useless. Batteries drained too quickly. Even the stars disappeared behind a ceiling of heavy clouds.

In the heart of the city, three people stood waiting.

They weren't chosen for their strength or wisdom—only for the promise the candlemaker saw in them.

"This night will not lift quickly," he said, as he placed a candle into each of their hands.

"I have entrusted you with these flames for a reason: use them well. What you do in the darkness will shape what remains when the dawn comes."

For a long moment, they all stood still, watching their flames tremble against the shadows.

The light felt small.

The night felt endless.

Each wondered what to do.

The first stared at his candle. Its wax was flawless, the flame steady and bright—*too beautiful,* he thought, *to keep to himself.*

He lifted it high, marveling at the way it caught the eyes of passersby.

"Look!" someone gasped. "*He has a light!*"

The man smiled, thinking perhaps this was the purpose of the gift: to bring joy, to inspire admiration, to gather a crowd.

Soon he began to experiment—spinning the candle in his fingers, tossing it into the air and catching it without snuffing the flame. He held it near his face as he spoke, letting its glow sharpen his expressions. People gathered. Applause rang out. Cheers rippled across the darkness, and for a while the night seemed less worrisome.

"More!" the crowd cried. "*Make it burn higher! Make it brighter!*"

Their demands fueled his ambition. He pressed the wick to burn hotter, shielded the flame with cupped hands against the wind, and doubled his tricks—burning through wax and time at a reckless pace.

But as the night wore on, he felt the candle shrinking in his grip. Hot wax spilled between his fingers, searing his skin. The flame sputtered, defiant at first, then faltering despite all his efforts to protect it.

One final toss. One desperate catch.

And then—the flame went out.

The applause faltered, the crowd shifted uneasily, already scanning the dark for another spectacle.

"*Is that it?*" someone called from the back.

The man stared at the charred stub in his palm as the night seemed to close in again, heavier than before.

The second man held his candle like a torch and walked with purpose.

He saw it not as a showpiece but as a tool—a way to push back the darkness.

This light isn't for me alone, he thought, tightening his grip on the wax as if the flame itself depended on his resolve.

He began to move with urgency—rushing from house to house, alley to alley, touching his flame to torches and lanterns. Each new spark brought a flicker of pride.

Ten. Twenty. Fifty.

He kept count in his mind, but he never lingered—there was always another wick waiting to be lit, another corner of darkness to conquer.

Driven by efficiency, he gathered people into groups, always aiming for the largest possible crowd. The bigger the group, the faster he could pass along the flame. As soon as the last wick caught, he moved on without a word, already searching for the next gathering to ignite.

But behind him, many fires flickered out—untended and forgotten. Others grew wild, burning hot and bright but all too briefly before dying in the night air.

His own candle, burning harder than he had planned, shrank faster than he could believe. He scraped at the soft wax with his thumb, trying to stretch it farther, whispering to himself, "*I must keep moving. There's still so much more to do.*"

By the time he reached the next street, there was nothing left—only blackened fingers, the faint smell of smoke, and a trail of scattered embers behind him where the darkness was already closing in again.

The third lingered where she was, holding her candle close enough to feel its warmth seep into her palms.

Its glow was small—barely enough to light the path at her feet. She studied the flicker and murmured to herself, "*Use it well.*"

But what that meant, she wasn't entirely sure.

She moved slowly, her steps careful and deliberate.

In the doorway of a shuttered shop, she noticed an old woman huddled against the cold, her shoulders hunched beneath a threadbare shawl. The woman cradled a candle of her own—burned halfway down, the wick stiff and dark, the wax hardened into a useless stub.

The girl knelt, lowering her light so the glow rested between them. The old woman looked up, her eyes tired and her hands trembling.

"*Take my flame,*" the girl said softly, extending her candle toward her.

The woman hesitated, shaking her head. "*I'm afraid it will go out again,*" she whispered. "*I don't know how to keep it going.*"

"*Then let's do it together,*" the girl answered, her voice warm and unhurried. "*I'll stay with you, however long it takes.*"

She guided the woman's hands, showing her how to tilt her candle just enough. The girl held her own steady, shielding the wick from the wind as the two candles met. For a breathless moment, the flame wavered—uncertain. Then it caught.

It was small at first, fragile against the night air, but together they cupped their palms around it until the light steadied.

When it finally held, the girl smiled and whispered, "*You can tend it now.*"

She rose and walked on, carrying her candle at the pace of grace.

With each person she encountered, she stayed long enough—long enough for their flames to catch, for their fear to ease, and for their confidence to grow before she moved on.

By the time her own candle burned low, the streets glowed softly. Hundreds of lights flickered in windows and doorways, carried by hands she had once warmed.

Across the streets and alleys, some people she had helped were now kneeling beside others, their flames cupped in gentle hands.

They whispered words of encouragement. They taught trembling fingers how to tend fragile wicks. They lingered as she had once lingered, waiting for each light to take hold.

A serene satisfaction spread across her face. She noticed her own flame was nearly gone.

But now, the light no longer depended on her.

THE KIND BEGGAR

We often celebrate acts of generosity that are large, public, and impressive—measured in money, followers, or media coverage. However, this story highlights something different. It's about what we value, what we hold back, and what it means to be truly generous when no one's watching.

Just then he (Jesus) looked up and saw the rich people dropping offerings in the collection plate. Then he saw a poor widow put in two pennies. He said, "The plain truth is that this widow has given by far the largest offering today. All these others made offerings that they'll never miss; she gave extravagantly what she couldn't afford—she gave her all!"

- Luke 21:1-4 (MSG)

From his corner on the cracked sidewalk, he watched the world rush past, blind to his presence.

He sat outside the coffeehouse, slumped against the wall like an abandoned backpack. His jacket had once been navy, but now it faded into the gray of the sidewalk itself. His shoes were patched with tape, three layers thick on the left one.

He didn't ask for anything. Didn't shake a cup or hold a sign. Only nodded faintly at the few who met his eyes—most didn't.

Every day, commuters, tourists, nurses on break, and kids skipping class streamed past—each guessing what he wanted. Most guessed wrong.

They guessed at his story, too. Some said he used to be a teacher. Others said a welder. Or a father who had lost a child and unraveled from the inside out. But stories linger longer when they stay vague, and in cities like this, compassion rarely stops moving.

He spotted her in the crowd before she even reached the corner.

There was nothing outwardly wrong with her appearance. Her blouse was neatly pressed. Sensible shoes. Hair pulled back—an effort at composure that revealed she hadn't had time to fuss.

What betrayed her wasn't how she looked, but how she carried herself. The manila folder in her arms was clutched too tightly—held to her chest as if it contained the last fragments of her life, as if letting go of it might make everything else come undone. She held it the way someone braces for an impact.

She didn't move like the others streaming down the street. They walked with a rhythm, a purpose. She drifted, as if wading through fog too thick to see what lay ahead. There was a hollow caution in her steps, a quiet stiffness that belonged to someone still navigating the shock of loss. Her eyes were glassy and unfocused—moving in slow motion against a world rushing past her.

Near the corner, she stopped. For a heartbeat, she tilted her face toward the sky as if offering a silent plea—asking for a reason to keep standing.

The folder in her grip looked thin, almost empty, yet she cradled it as though it bore the heaviness of everything she had just lost. She blinked hard, trying to will the tears back into hiding. But one escaped, tracing a silent path down her cheek. Then another followed. And another.

That's when he felt it—faint yet insistent, a nudge he couldn't explain and couldn't ignore. It wasn't pity; it was recognition. As if something in her sorrow had reached out and brushed against his own.

His hand slipped into his coat as if searching for an answer he knew he wouldn't find. His fingers closed around the crumpled paper bag in his inside pocket. He hesitated, thumb rubbing over the thin paper as if it might tell him what to do.

Inside were two sealed peanut-butter crackers and a single five-dollar bill—his entire week folded into a bag no bigger than his fist. He'd been saving the crackers, not just for hunger but for Friday, when the shelter's line would snake around the block and the soup pot would run dry. Those crackers had been his quiet assurance that he wouldn't be forgotten.

He pulled the bag halfway out, then stopped. He wasn't sure if it was kindness or desperation guiding his hand. What could two crackers possibly do for her?

His stomach clenched, already bargaining with him: *You'll need them. You barely have enough for yourself.*

But when he looked at her again—at the way she clutched that thin folder to her chest as though it were the last piece of her life, at the tear slipping down her cheek as she tried to hide it—something in him wouldn't stay silent.

He wanted to reach her, to somehow say, *I see you... you're not invisible.* But another thought pressed in just as sharply: he didn't want to frighten her. A stranger stepping out of the shadows—especially one with a torn coat, weathered face, and the look of someone who had slept outside too many nights—could feel like another threat in a day already too heavy to bear.

So he lingered there on the edge of the moment, torn between the pull to keep his small security and the deeper pull to let her know she was seen. The bag in his hand wasn't really the gift. The gift was in breaking the silence, in daring to bridge the distance the world had left around her.

He stood slowly, his knees popping like gravel, and crossed toward her. She didn't see him at first. When he held out the bag, she blinked in confusion.

"*You dropped something,*" he said as tenderly as he could, keeping his voice low so as not to startle her.

She glanced down at the ground, puzzled. "*I didn't...*" Her words faded as her eyes searched the pavement.

"*It's okay,*" he added, his tone gentle as he extended his hand and pressed the small paper bag into hers. "*It's yours now.*"

She looked at him—really looked this time. Her gaze lingered on his cracked lips, the sunken cheeks shadowed by a rough beard, the threadbare gloves that barely covered his fingers. Something in her expression shifted from confusion to ache.

"*I can't take this,*" she said, pushing the bag back toward him. "*You need this more than I do.*"

His gaze fell to the sidewalk. "*Maybe... maybe not.*" He paused, as if weighing something heavier than the bag. His voice softened, almost fragile. "*But I know what it's like to need more than food...*" He reached out, barely brushing her sleeve—just the faintest touch, as though asking permission to close the space between them. "*...to know you're not alone.*"

For a moment, she glimpsed something beyond his worn face—an unshakable light no hunger could dim. And that light unsettled her—something steady, kind, and unbroken, as if he carried a richness no poverty could take away. She didn't have a response to his radical act of generosity—only tears.

She clutched the bag as though it were sacred, though it wasn't the bag that moved her but his kindness—the way it had seen her when no one else did.

She held the bag close, tears still streaking her cheeks, and stepped back into the current of the street. To anyone else, she was just another passerby. But she walked away as if she had touched something holy.

He returned to his spot. His coat felt heavier without the bag in it, and the ache in his stomach grew sharper. Still, he sat the same way he always had—quiet, still, unnoticed.

The next morning, she came back. She didn't know why. Maybe to thank him. Maybe to offer something in return. Maybe because something inside her needed to see if he had been there at all. But the corner was empty.

She came again the next day. And the next. Each time, she walked a little slower, lingered a little longer—always hoping.

He was gone.

She thought of him often—the man in the fraying coat who, without spotlight or applause, had given all he had. She remembered the warmth of the crackers still in the bag, the quiet firmness in his voice, the way he had looked at her without pity. She wondered where he had gone. Had anyone else ever noticed him?

And the truth was, she hadn't been the only one who saw him that day.

Heaven had been walking those streets all along—silent, unseen... smiling.

THE SONG BENEATH THE CITY

Sometimes we sense something just beneath the surface of our lives—an ache, a pull, a flicker of meaning we can't quite explain. It can show up in quiet moments, unexpected beauty, or a sudden longing we don't have words for. We try to brush it off, to keep pace with everything that demands our attention. But what if that tug we feel is not a distraction... but an invitation? What if something more profound is calling to us, not with answers, but is the answer itself?

"Whoever has ears to hear, let them hear."

-(Jesus) Matthew 11:15 (NIV)

Most people never heard the music.

The city was far too loud—engines growled, horns blared, and billboards screamed for attention. The streets pulsed with urgency. Everyone had somewhere to be, something to prove. Life moved fast; to pause was to fall behind, and even slowing for a breath might look like weakness.

But beneath the concrete and chaos—beneath the rush and ritual—there was a song. Not broadcast. Not advertised. It came from nowhere, and from everywhere at once. It seeped through subway grates, threaded up sidewalk cracks, climbed through rusted vents and forgotten shafts, and resonated in the silence of neglected alleyways.

The song was faint—so faint that even those who heard it weren't entirely sure they'd heard anything at all. It wasn't a melody you could hum, nor a lyric you could sing. It was a presence in the form of sound: ancient, honest, and sacred. Most people walked past it without a second thought.

But not everyone.

A few—just a few—would pause mid-stride and tilt their heads slightly, as if some forgotten memory had brushed their shoulder. They didn't know why they'd stopped, only that something had reached through the noise and numbness and touched them—something that slipped between the cracks of their carefully ordered lives and stirred something they'd nearly forgotten was there.

It called to them—not loudly, but clearly.

For most, it was only a moment. They shook it off, blaming it on fatigue or distraction, and kept walking.

For some, it was enough to unsettle the rhythm of their routine—enough to make them wonder, enough to make them listen. And when they really listened, they didn't just hear it in their ears; they felt it in their chests.

There was hesitation, of course—doubt and fear. *Who leaves what's normal to chase what no one else seems to hear?*

There were no signs, only whispers—soft as breath against the ear::

"Keep going."

"I am with you."

"This way."

Compelled by something they couldn't explain, they left the crowded streets and turned down empty alleyways that reeked of rust and old regrets. They entered stairwells that descended into stations long since closed. They stepped over broken signs, ducked beneath fences marked with warnings, and passed places where others had long since stopped looking.

People noticed. *"You okay?"* some asked. *"You're chasing shadows. Don't waste your life on something that isn't real."*

But the ones who had heard the song couldn't unhear it. It had woven itself into them. It knew them—each one. It knew their fatigue, their failures, their secret ache for something more.

The song continued to play, growing stronger as the listeners moved toward it. The journey led through places most people avoided—utility tunnels, abandoned corridors, forgotten systems buried beneath progress.

It wasn't clean. It wasn't glamorous. Still, each grimy step carried the quiet certainty that they were moving toward something true.

They noticed strange things: flickers of light where no power ran, corners where the air smelled of rain instead of rot. In places where nothing should live, green vines climbed cracked stone—stubborn, unexpected, and in bloom.

And always, always, the song—closer now, louder, not from above or below, but from within.

They started to understand. The song wasn't just luring them into mystery; it was leading them into meaning. It didn't demand they understand it before they followed—it simply invited them. And the deeper they went, the more their fears fell away. The path remained difficult and dangerous, but their hearts were growing braver.

The song changed them the further they went—or perhaps it awakened the part of them that had always longed to be found.

Then one day—without fanfare or final step—they simply arrived where the song had always begun.

There were no signs, no applause—just a stillness filled with sound. They stood there, tired and stained by the city above, yet somehow whole. The song surrounded them.

Then slowly, it began to sing through them—not with their mouths, but with their lives.

Wherever they moved, the sound they had once followed now moved through them. It hummed in the way they looked at people. It resonated in their kindness. It pulsed in their patience.

When they returned to the world above, people sometimes stared—not at them exactly, but at something they couldn't name. They looked different. Not dramatic. Not polished or perfect. But they seemed grounded, at peace with themselves and with those around them.

It was as if the song had etched itself into their essence. There was clarity in their eyes, as if they were seeing with both softness and strength. They smiled more, but not as a performance. They moved more slowly, but with purpose. They spoke less, but their words carried weight.

They gave others their full attention—holding doors a little longer, laughing without sarcasm, listening without interrupting, weeping without shame.

Some said they just felt safe standing near them—like everything was going to be okay, no matter what. The song resonated within them—gently, steadily, boldly—shaping the way they moved through the world.

Once in a while, someone on the busy street pauses, tilts their head as if catching a distant melody, and whispers:

"Do you hear that?"

THE PLASTIC TREE

We all know what it feels like to keep something alive long after it's lost its soul—a relationship that looks perfect on the outside but is quietly falling apart, a career that once lit you up but now wears you down, a version of yourself you present to the world while something inside feels quietly absent. We polish, we pretend, we push through. But eventually, the fractures show—and what we do next reveals what we truly value: the truth of who we really are.

"These people make a big show of saying the right thing, but their heart isn't in it."

- Jesus (Matthew 15:8) MSG

The tree in the town park was magnificent—so magnificent that it made the town famous.

Every spring, people traveled from miles around to see it. Its vibrant colors and fragrant blossoms made it the centerpiece of the park—a towering, breathtaking presence with branches heavy with blooms that swayed like gentle sighs in the wind.

It had become more than a tree. It was a tradition, a symbol... a brand.

Postcards featured its silhouette against golden sunsets. Couples proposed beneath its canopy. Parents named their children after the flowers it bloomed. Local businesses used it in their logos. Organizers scheduled festivals to coincide with its blossoms. The tree was more than just an attraction; it was embedded in the town's identity.

One spring, something unexpected happened.

The tree remained bare—its branches stiff and gray, as if winter had refused to let go. No buds unfurled to promise new life. No blossoms opened to perfume the breeze. No bursts of color shimmered against the sky. The season that once turned the park into a living festival arrived in silence, leaving the tree standing stark and still, like a shadow of the life it once carried..

The town council commissioned the Parks Department to investigate. They tested the soil, scraped bark, and examined branches. What they discovered unsettled them.

The soil beneath the tree had long been drained of life. The roots, once strong and healthy, were riddled with decay. Slowly and quietly, the tree had been dying for years—hidden beneath the surface, ignored until it was too late. Regardless, the life that had once pulsed through its veins had ceased.

When the town council learned the truth, they panicked. Not publicly, of course. Publicly, they smiled and reassured concerned citizens:

"*It's only a late bloom,*" one councilman said with a well-rehearsed grin.

"*Tourists will stop coming,*" another warned. "*Photographers will move on to other landmarks.*"

"*We can't risk it,*" the mayor concluded, tapping the table.

Since they couldn't save the tree, they decided to maintain the image.

They secretly hired artists to repaint the leaves in a brighter, more vibrant green. They attached silk blossoms to the branches, each one delicately handcrafted and carefully arranged to match last year's photos. Hidden speakers were placed in the bushes to play a loop of bird songs, and every morning before the park opened, workers sprayed floral perfume into the air. New signs were installed at the entrance, cheerfully proclaiming:

ENJOY THE BLOSSOMS!

For a time, it worked.

Visitors returned in droves. The tree looked alive—perhaps even more perfect than before. Posts and hashtags flooded social media, and local shops saw their profits rise. The illusion held.

But something was wrong. Children reached out to touch the petals, and the petals didn't move. "*Why doesn't it smell real?*" a few asked. Birds stopped coming. The wind, once playful among the branches, passed through with no response. The shimmer remained, but the soul was gone.

People sensed it, even if they couldn't explain it. Something about the tree felt off—too flawless, too still to be alive.

Still, the town council pressed on, committed to the illusion.

"*Everything's fine,*" one councilman insisted when rumors surfaced, waving away concern.

Dissenting voices were quieted with reassurances and distractions.

They added more silk blossoms. More perfume. More polish. They weren't preserving a tree. They were curating a myth.

Then came the next winter. A violent blizzard rolled through the region, dropping temperatures to record lows. Gale-force winds tore through the park, driving snow sideways, rattling signs, and bending even the sturdiest trees. In the storm's fury, the tree groaned under the strain before the trunk gave a hollow crack, splitting in two as the upper half collapsed into the snow with a dull, lifeless thud.

By morning, the town had gathered to assess the damage. The branch lay twisted and broken across the frozen path. Children stared. Tourists took pictures. But it was what lay beneath the break that silenced everyone.

The branch's core was hollow—not merely weakened, but empty. The once-mighty tree had rotted from the inside out. Only the shell remained—painted, perfumed, and polished.

There were no words—just the cold hum of realization. The tree, for all its grandeur, had died long ago. Instead of mourning it, the town council embalmed it—dressing it up as a display to keep up appearances.

Some wept quietly, their tears falling for what had been lost. Others raged at the years of deception. But most simply turned away, unwilling to look upon the hollow shell of what they once revered. Their silence carried a heavier weight than any accusation.

In the end, nothing remained but the exposed truth—undeniable, unadorned, and impossible to ignore.

THE QUESTION

Life hands us three questions that drive nearly everything we do:

Who am I?

Why am I here?

Where do I belong?

But there is a deeper question still—one that must be answered first. Because without it, even our best pursuits eventually run into dead ends. This question isn't about religion or rituals. It's more personal than that. It's about a person who, even if you don't know his name yet, he knows yours.

"And how about you? Who do you say I am?"

- (Jesus) Matthew 16:15 (NIV)

He had wandered the street market for as long as he could remember.

It wasn't a market of bread or cloth, but of questions—advertised on chalkboards, neon banners, and glossy flyers fluttering beneath folding tents. QR codes promised answers with a single scan. Voices clamored, each vendor's claim more insistent than the last.

"Searching for significance? Scan here for your free quiz!"

"Lost your direction? Download our app—your life will never be the same!"

"Feeling like a misfit? Subscribe now—belong somewhere bigger!"

The wanderer moved among them, weary yet unwilling to stop. At first, he believed them all. He paid dearly—time, energy, even fragments of his heart—for the trinkets and tools they offered.

The first was a mirror—a cracked fragment, actually. Small enough to fit in his hand.

"This will reveal who you truly are," the vendor promised.

But the reflection was splintered. Some days he appeared strong and radiant; other days, cracked and twisted.

One night, in despair, the mirror slipped from his grasp, and shattered. He tried to piece it back together, but the cracks only multiplied.

He returned to the market a few weeks later, clutching the broken shard. The vendors were louder. So were his doubts. But he kept moving.

Next came a map, intricate and beautiful, purchased from a table draped in patterned scarves and LED string lights.

"Follow this, and you'll find your destiny," the mapmaker assured him.

The wanderer traced the map's path, hiking valleys of opportunity and climbing mountains of achievement. But no matter how far he walked, every trail looped back to where he began. The lines felt endless, like a maze without an exit.

Months passed before he wandered back, map in hand, worn and creased. The same promises echoed from new voices. He tried not to listen. But hope—however fragile—pulled him toward them.

Finally, he received a brass key from a confident woman with a polished sales pitch.

"With this, you will unlock your place in the world," she said, her voice smooth and persuasive.

He carried it close, gripping it tight as he tried door after door—some too grand to enter, some too strange to understand. Yet every lock resisted him. The doors remained cold and unmoved.

He nearly gave up. But the market's noise, its motion, its shimmering offers—it kept luring him back. He didn't believe any of it anymore, not really. But he didn't know where else to go.

When he finally returned, his eyes were darker. His steps slower. The mirror shard, the map, and the brass key all weighed him down now—not with promise, but with failure.

Now, at the market's edge, he stood trembling, feet throbbing, shoulders sagging under the weight of a faded map, a jagged mirror shard, and a brass key grown heavy in his hand.

The vendors' cries had dulled to murmurs behind him, their bright colors bleeding into gray. He had run out of promises to chase.

And then... he saw him.

It wasn't the first time. The man always sat quietly at the edge of the street, not far from the last vendor—but not one of them. No signs. No table. No noise. He simply sat there as though waiting for someone who hadn't yet arrived.

The wanderer remembered passing him before, dismissing him as just another merchant. But this man had no sign, no prices, no eager call to draw him in.

Rumors stirred in the wanderer's memory—some said the man was a prophet, others a fraud. They claimed he could see straight through you, down to the places you hid from yourself. Some walked away exposed and angry. Others... others left different.

The vendors never spoke of him, yet their silence felt deliberate, as if children pretending not to notice a storm gathering on the horizon.

Now the man was watching the worn-out wanderer. His gaze was calm, unhurried, but carried a quiet authority too heavy to name. The wanderer's chest tightened. *Surely this is another trap*, he thought. *But what if... it's not?*

Hesitant, he stepped closer. The man gestured to the empty bench beside him, and the wanderer sat. For a long moment neither spoke. Yet the silence felt strangely alive—not awkward, not oppressive—almost as if the world itself were holding its breath.

The quiet man's eyes shifted to the mirror shard in the wanderer's hand. "*You've been searching for yourself in that reflection,*" he said, his voice clear and confident.

The wanderer nodded. "*I thought it would tell me who I am...*" His voice cracked as he lowered his gaze. "*...but now all I see are the cracks.*"

"*And the map?*" the man asked, glancing toward the parchment tucked beneath the young man's arm. "*How far has it taken you?*"

"*Far,*" the wanderer admitted. "*I've walked until my feet bled. But every road circles back. I'm still lost.*"

At last, the man's eyes fell on the brass key clenched in the wanderer's other hand. "*You've tried the doors?*"

"*Yes. All of them,*" the wanderer said, rubbing the key in his palm. "*Some wouldn't open. Others... led to places where I didn't belong. I'm still locked out.*"

The words caught in his throat, and he swallowed hard. "*I thought these would give me the answers... but I'm still empty.*"

The quiet man's face softened—not with pity, but with a fierce, unshakable compassion. He leaned in slightly. "*What if I told you the answers aren't in the mirror, or the map, or even the key?*"

The wanderer frowned, scanning the stalls as if the answer might be hidden among them. "*Then where?*" he asked.

The quiet man's eyes met his, steady and unblinking, his voice low but carrying a weight that settled over the wanderer like a mantle. "*I am the mirror that can reveal who you truly are,*" he began, his voice even and measured. "*I am the map that leads you* into your purpose. And I am the key that opens the door to where you belong."

The words sank deep, rippling outward until they touched hidden places the wanderer didn't know existed. His chest tightened. His pulse pounded. He swallowed hard, searching for something—anything—to say. When his voice came, it was small. "Look, I can tell... you're a good and wise man..." It was a polite attempt to end a conversation that had gone too deep.

But the quiet man leaned forward, interrupting him gently, his tone unwavering. "Only God is truly good," he said, his voice full of quiet reverence. "There is no good apart from Him."

A quiet joy rose behind his eyes—deep, steady, unmistakable. "Every kindness you've felt... every breath of beauty... every moment of peace—it all flows from Him and nowhere else."

The wanderer's pulse quickened. The man's voice carried on, low and deliberate, as though reciting a poem etched into eternity. "All wisdom is from God too. Every truth that has ever set a heart free... every insight that has ever lit a dark path—it all begins and ends with Him."

Then his tone shifted—still calm, but unflinching. "I've told you who I am," he said, his voice unshaken. "If you think I'm lying, then I am evil. If you think I'm delusional, then I'm a fool. But you cannot call me 'good' or 'wise' unless you consider the only other possibility."

The noise of the market seemed to fade as if the world itself had grown still. The wanderer felt the weight of the words press in on his chest. Still, he had to ask. "What other possibility?"

The man's eyes rested on him—sure, unshaken, as if he already knew him. Yet there was no judgment in them, only a strange, disarming kindness. "*I am who I say I am.*"

His words lingered in the air, leaving a silence that felt spacious, as though the world had stepped aside to let their weight settle. The wanderer had spent his life searching—who he was, why he was here, where he belonged—yet the answers always slipped away. Perhaps he had been asking the wrong questions all along.

As the man's statement sank in, something stirred within him—not from pressure but from recognition, like wounds responding to a healer's touch. The breeze stilled around them, and the quiet man leaned in again. "*One question holds every answer you seek.*"

The words didn't press on the wanderer; they brushed against a hidden longing, awakening the ache to know what question could hold such weight.

"*What is the question?*" he asked, his voice edged with urgency.

The quiet man's gaze held steady, leaning in as if about to reveal the very meaning of life:

"*Who do you... say I am?*"

THE HEALING CLINIC

Not all illnesses begin with pain. Some arrive quietly, disguised as stress or exhaustion, slowly taking hold beneath the surface of a busy, managed life. The world offers treatments—distractions, affirmations, routines—to ease the discomfort without naming the cause. But somewhere, beyond the noise and ease, a place remains where we can see the actual disease for what it is... and heal it at the cost of surrender.

"Who needs a doctor: the healthy or the sick? I'm here inviting outsiders, not insiders—an invitation to a changed life, changed inside and out."

- Jesus (Luke 5:31,32) MSG

They didn't know they were dying.

Or maybe they did and were simply in denial.

The signs were subtle—numbness, a weariness no rest could touch, a hidden weight behind every smile. Easy to blame it on stress, strained relationships, or just an awful week.

Everyone felt it, so no one questioned it.

There was a clinic downtown—bright, clean, and always open. The doctors wore polished shoes and calming smiles. They listened well, nodded often, and prescribed just enough to keep things manageable. For the restlessness, a change of routine. For the apathy, a new playlist. For the emptiness, a self-help book, or maybe just a scented candle.

And for the fear that stirred beneath it all... well, they offered only words. Polished words. Words like *resilience*, *self-care*, and *mindfulness*. Words that soothed for a while but never healed..

No one dared speak of the deeper disease—neither patient nor staff. Naming it would require facing it. And facing it would mean admitting it was real. Besides, it was easier to treat symptoms than confront causes. It was so much easier to stay productive than pause long enough to ask why.

The clinic became a refuge where no one had to look too closely or feel too deeply. People returned again and again—grateful, even loyal. Their files thickened, prescriptions multiplied. They smiled through the strain, convinced they were improving. After all, they didn't feel as bad as before.

They wanted to believe they were healing. But after a while, they felt worse and returned to the clinic.

Across the city, down an aging street of leaning buildings, stood another place. It bore no logo, only a wooden door with a small brass plate that read: *Healer.*

Few entered. Fewer stayed.

The room inside was stark—bare walls, pale light, and the hollow echo of footsteps on linoleum. There was no soft waiting music to soothe the nerves, no framed posters urging anyone to *be their best self*, no cheerful slogans congratulating patients for their bravery in showing up.

Only a quiet presence lingered—almost tangible—and eyes that seemed to see too much. The Healer who waited within didn't bother with surface-level comfort. He didn't treat symptoms. He named the disease for what it was. And unlike anyone before him, he carried the cure.

The cure wasn't painless—neither polished nor pleasant. It stripped away pretense. It pulled shame into the light. Not cruelly, but honestly. And not everyone wanted that. Some came once and never returned. Others lingered by the door but stepped away before it opened.

One woman—a regular at the downtown clinic—found herself at that door one cold morning. Her usual strategies had stopped working. The doctors' words rang hollow. The distractions left her emptier than before. A quiet dread was seeping somewhere beneath the surface.

She had heard rumors about the Healer. Fragments of overheard conversations. Scribbled notes tucked into forgotten corners. They all said the same thing: *He doesn't soothe the symptoms. He cures the cause.*

Still she hesitated, fearing he would name what she had avoided for years—that her problem wasn't seasonal or circumstantial. That it wasn't something to manage—it was something to surrender.

And the pressure inside her rose—not just emotionally, but spiritually. What if the ache was keeping her from something deeper? What if naming the disease made it more real? What if she wasn't ready to let go of the life she had crafted around hiding it?

She knocked.

The door opened instantly, as if he had been waiting for her all along. His eyes found hers before she could speak—eyes that seemed to reach past the surface, past the weary lines on her face, past the cloud of doubt and the tremor of fear beneath her composure. He asked no questions. He simply stepped aside and invited her in.

When he placed his hand gently over her heart, she felt it—an awareness that pierced deeper than words. It wasn't stress. It wasn't a breakdown. Not burnout or imbalance. This went further, buried beneath the layers she had blamed for so long. It was older. It was rooted in her very nature, something that had seeped into her soul.

He named it—not a clinical label but a word as ancient as the ache itself. A word she had half-suspected yet never dared to speak:

Death—that had begun in the soul and was reaching for the rest of her.

The words undid her. She wept—and he wept with her. Not out of pity, but with a grief strangely shared.

Then, in the quiet that followed, he offered the cure. It wasn't a pill. It wasn't a new pathway or the promise of a fresh program.

The cure was himself—an unfathomable exchange: *his life for hers, her life for his.*

Her throat constricted until breath itself felt trapped. A torrent of questions thundered through her mind, a river breaking its dam.

"Who are you... *who are you to even say something like that?*" The words tumbled out raw and uneven. Her breath hitched as another thought clawed its way to the surface.

"What are you giving me? I don't..."

Her voice faltered and broke. Her eyes darted to the corners of the room—the bare walls, the still air—searching for footing anywhere but in his eyes. She thought of running, of fleeing as far as she could from this place, but there was nowhere else to go. She groped for words, for something solid to grasp, yet every question only splintered into another.

"I *don't understand,*" she finally said, the words small and hoarse. "How *could that possibly heal my disease?*"

At last, her gaze returned to him. There was compassion in his eyes, but also something heavier—an ache that felt as though her suffering had crossed the space between them and taken root in him.

Her breath trembled. Deeper questions rose from places she had tried to bury, cutting closer to the bone than she wanted to admit. Her words came out jagged, almost breaking apart on her lips.

"Why... *would you ever trade your life for mine? Why? What makes me so worth... that?*"

He looked at her as though he could see every moment she

had ever lived—each secret, each sorrow, each fleeting joy. The weight of his gaze left her feeling utterly exposed, yet, to her surprise, it carried no threat. Instead, beneath that unspoken knowing, she felt a strange and unexpected safety.

When he finally answered, his voice was steady, quiet enough to draw her closer without moving at all.

"*Because your very existence matters so much to me,*" he said, the words falling like a confession. "*I will give myself... to set you free.*"

She searched his face for answers she could measure, verify, control. There were none. Only a certainty in his eyes—a certainty that didn't demand her comprehension, only her trust.

She would have to believe him without having all the answers. She didn't understand it. She couldn't. But she knew enough: the disease was real, but so was he.

"*If you give your life to me,*" she said, the ache in her voice unmistakable. "*What happens when someone else comes? How can you keep offering it?*"

He responded with quiet authority. "*Because the disease you carry has no power over me. I've already passed through death—and undone it.*"

It didn't make sense at all. It wasn't logical. Honestly, it sounded insane.

Yet, somehow she believed him. She couldn't explain why—whether it was born of desperation or something deeper. All she knew was that she trusted him. She had to.

A quiet faith welled up inside her, one that defied every rational voice in her head. It rose above her doubts like a whisper cutting through the storm. Even so, she knew it was true.

She thought of his words—*a trade; his life for hers, her life for his.*

Her breath shook as her eyes met his.

"Yes," she said softly, the word barely more than a breath.

It hurt. Surrender always does. Healing does too. But in the very moment his life became hers, the disease loosened its grip.

She felt it—an unseen unraveling, as if invisible cords were loosening one by one. She felt the cleansing sweep through her, not as water on the skin but as light seeping into the hidden places within her soul. She felt the change—quiet but undeniable—like something old breaking apart to make room for something new.

She left the clinic whole—imperfect, yet free.

When she spoke of her healing, many refused to believe her.

"Her naivete," they scoffed, "*made her a pawn in a cruel game of manipulation.*"

Some dismissed her story with a casual wave.

"*She was never that sick to begin with,*" they concluded.

So they went back to their previous clinic—grateful for their distractions, content to smile through their numbness, thanking their doctors for yet another day of temporary relief, even as the deeper disease advanced unseen.

But a few... a few leaned in and listened. They came to the Healer—hesitant at first, then desperate enough to step through the wooden door. One by one, they entered the small, unadorned room. And each one who laid down their pride and took up his life walked out healed.

The downtown clinic still thrives—busy as ever, with a waiting list to prove it.

But down the quiet street, the wooden door still waits.

And the Healer still answers every knock.

THE ENTRANCE EXAM

From the time we're young, we're taught that life rewards effort. Work hard enough, check all the right boxes, and you'll earn your place. It feels like every door worth opening requires proof that you deserve it. But what if there's a door where none of that applies? What if the thing that matters most isn't how impressive your list is—but whether you're willing to lay it down?

Saving is all his idea, and all his work. All we do is trust him enough to let him do it. It's God's gift from start to finish! We don't play the major role. If we did, we'd probably go around bragging that we'd done the whole thing! No, we neither make nor save ourselves. God does both the making and saving.

- Ephesians 2:8,9 (MSG)

They told him there would be only one question. Just one. His answer would decide everything.

That's all he remembered as he stepped into the room—white walls, white desk, white chair. Stark and silent. The only color came from the graphite pencil on the desk and the single line of text at the top of the page:

Why should you be admitted?

The question stared back at him, unblinking.

He wasn't alone. Rows of people filled the room, seated in identical chairs at identical desks, each facing the same question. But if the prompt was the same, the answers being written around him could not have been more different.

As soon as the test began, pencils moved with purpose. Some wrote in sweeping strokes, as if they'd rehearsed for this moment their entire lives. Others paused briefly, then constructed careful sentences—measured, deliberate, confident.

No one hesitated long. They all seemed to know exactly what to say.

But he didn't. Not at first.

He re-read the question, again and again:

Why should you be admitted?

Everyone else appeared to arrive with an answer already formed. Business suits, flowing dresses, cardigan sweaters—clothing that suggested they belonged. Their posture radiated self-assurance. Their calm expressions hinted that the outcome was merely a formality.

A woman near the front underlined her last sentence with a decisive flourish. Even from a distance, he could almost read the confidence in her words:

I've always done the right thing.
I've lived with integrity.
I've treated others the way I wanted to be treated.

The man beside him built a methodical list:

Donated to charity.
Volunteered every weekend.
Never lied, never cheated, never stole.

Even their handwriting looked confident, precise, and sure.

The room hummed with the sound of people proving themselves: pencils scratching, pages turning, the soft rustle of papers being squared neatly in place.

He glanced down at the blank page in front of him. He felt smaller than his chair. Smaller than the question.

He had done nothing spectacular. Not awful, but not remarkable either. Some decent moments, maybe. But mostly forgettable. He could have written something safe—something polished and vaguely admirable.

But as he raised the pencil, his stomach knotted. Pretending felt hollow.

Then came the regrets—rising up from every corner of his memory, like skeletons crawling up out of the ground.

He saw arguments left unresolved.
He remembered faces he'd walked away from:

The ones he used.

The ones he ignored.

The ones he wounded—both deliberately and carelessly.

There were the lies—so many lies.

Some told to protect his image, others to shield himself from pain.

And some spoken simply because they were easier than the truth.

He recalled the rage that had erupted in the hidden places of his heart.

The countless excuses he made for never attempting to bring healing.

The humiliating secrets he still prayed no one would ever discover.

Whole seasons of his life stood marked by selfishness.

Entire chapters felt too shameful ever to be read aloud.

He clenched the pencil. His hand was shaking.

He looked around again. Some had finished and were rereading their essays with quiet pride. A young man adjusted his collar, satisfied with his clever phrasing. Across the aisle, a woman sat with her hands folded, radiating poise.

He wished he could be like them. To craft a story with just the right balance of virtue and humility—impressive yet modest.

But something in him wouldn't let him lie. He looked down at the page again. Then lowered his head. He wrote a single sentence:

I don't deserve to be here.

That was all. No defense. No spin.

Just honesty... and the expectation that it would immediately disqualify him from entering.

He set the pencil down and closed his eyes.

Then—softly, almost soundlessly—a note appeared on his desk. White, edged in gold. Embossed with a crest. A single word written in elegant script:

ACCEPTED.

He blinked and slowly reached out, afraid it might be a mistake and that it would be taken away.

Around him, heads turned. Stares sharpened. Murmurs stirred like wind across dry grass.

"What did you write?"

"That's not fair."

"That's not even an answer."

He shook his head—barely—less in defense than in wonder.

A man nearby snatched up his paper and began rewriting furiously. Others followed, flipping pages, lengthening lists, making their words bolder.

Some tore up their first attempts and started over, more determined than before. The scratching of pencils returned—louder now. Urgent and desperate.

But no other envelopes appeared.

He stood quietly, letter in hand. His chair groaned softly as he stepped away.

No one followed.

He walked toward the door—the one no one else had dared approach. It opened easily. He paused for a moment at the threshold and glanced back.

Even now, they were bent over their papers, striving to impress—still trying to prove something that could never be earned.

They didn't look up. They didn't see him leave.

He stepped through the door and let it close quietly behind him.

The scratching of pencils grew louder.

THE SEWAGE TEST

We all draw invisible lines—between good and bad, clean and dirty, safe and unsafe. Most of the time, we trust our instincts to tell us when something crosses the line. But what happens when the line isn't where we thought it was? What if the standard we've been measuring ourselves by isn't the one that truly matters? Sometimes, it only takes one unsettling question to reveal just how close—or far—we really are.

We're all sin-infected, sin-contaminated. Our best efforts are grease-stained rags. We dry up like autumn leaves—sin-dried, we're blown off by the wind.

- Isaiah 64:6 (MSG)

It began as a casual dinner conversation between two friends—nothing planned, just catching up at the kitchen table over a coffee and a tea. Their talk drifted easily at first—harmless observations, laughter over shared memories, light thoughts about life's twists and turns.

But soon the conversation wandered toward the past—people they used to know, lives they'd once shared, those who had changed, and those who hadn't. Then, almost unexpectedly, the subject turned toward Heaven. Not in a preachy way. Just a quiet wondering.

"*I think God would be happy with how my life has gone,*" he said, almost offhand. "*I mean, I'm not perfect… but I think I'm a good enough person.*"

She raised an eyebrow and took a slow sip of her Earl Grey. Silence had always lingered comfortably between them. Her stillness nudged him to go on.

"*Well… I'm better than I used to be. Better than a lot of people, if I'm honest.*" He tried to laugh, but it landed flat.

She leaned back slightly in her chair, studying him. "*Better? Compared to whom?*"

He shrugged. "*I don't know. Just… people. Nobody gets it all right.*"

He lowered his gaze into his coffee cup as if he could hide in the swirl of liquid.

"*What if the standard isn't other people?*" she asked quietly. "*What if the standard is God?*"

He gave another shrug, trying to mask the unease that rose in his chest. "*I think I'm good enough for God. I mean, he knows my heart, right?"*

A trace of amusement flickered across her face before she spoke again. *"Yeah, he does."*

Without another word, she stood and disappeared into the kitchen. He tilted his head, puzzled, but didn't move. A moment later came the clink of glasses and the rush of running water.

She returned with a tray of five full drinking glasses, setting them in a neat row across the table like a science experiment.

"Let's say you're thirsty," she said, settling into her chair again. *"Really thirsty—and these are your only options."*

He leaned forward, curious. The first glass was thick and dark—mud-brown, with flecks clinging to the sides. A foul odor hit his nose before he even leaned closer.

"This one's fifty percent sewage," she explained. *"But it's fifty percent clean."*

"Are you serious? Of course I wouldn't drink it."

She nodded and motioned to the next. This one was slightly lighter but still cloudy and offensive.

"This one's twenty-five percent. Still toxic, just... diluted."

"Still no." He grimaced, pulling back.

The third glass looked like river water after a storm—murky, yellow-gray.

"Ten percent," she said. *"Not as obvious, but you'd know soon enough."*

He didn't reach for it.

The fourth looked almost normal—until one looked closely. A faint greenish tint floated beneath the surface, hard to notice unless you really looked.

"One percent," she said.

Then came the fifth. It looked perfect—clear as air. Light passed through it cleanly. No odor. No visible flaw.

"Point-zero-one percent. Almost nothing—practically perfect."

He stared at it. "How would someone even know?"

"They wouldn't," she replied. "Not right away."

Then, without a word, she slid the tray closer to his side of the table.

"Pick one," she said.

"You're out of your mind."

"If you had to drink one, which would it be?"

"None. I'm not drinking sewage." His laugh was uneasy.

She didn't push, but she didn't blink either.

He pointed reluctantly at the last glass. "That one looks clean. But if you say there's even a trace—no thanks."

"And why not?" she asked with a small smile.

"Because it's still in there. It doesn't matter how little—I'd never risk it."

She nodded slowly, letting his words hang between them. Then she leaned back, content to let the silence do the rest.

The ticking of the kitchen clock grew louder. The hum of the fridge seemed to join in. He sat staring at the fifth glass. It looked perfect—but now that he knew, he couldn't unsee it.

After a moment she spoke, her voice soft. *"Once you realize what's in the water—even a drop—'almost clean' never feels clean enough again."*

His voice dropped, carrying a new weight of unease. *"If God expects nothing less than perfection, how could anyone ever meet his standard?"*

He searched her face for an answer that wouldn't crush him. What he found wasn't judgment but compassion—followed by something stronger.

It was hope.

"One did," she said, holding his gaze. *"He drank it all—the sewage of our sin—yours and mine, so we wouldn't have to."*

He didn't reply. Not right away.

His eyes drifted back to the row of glasses—untouched but unforgettable. He knew he'd never look at a glass of water the same way again.

THE UNFINISHED STORY

At some point, we all wonder what our lives are really about. Are we just reacting to whatever comes our way? Trying to fit in or live up to what others expect? Or could there be a deeper story—one that's already been written for us, just waiting to be discovered? Maybe something inside us responds to a voice we don't fully understand, yet somehow recognize. And what if that voice isn't asking us to be perfect—but inviting us into something real, full of meaning and peace? This final parable is an invitation to pause, to listen, and to consider following the one who's known your name from the very beginning.

God can do anything, you know - far more than you could ever imagine or guess or request in your wildest dreams!

- Ephesians 3:20 (MSG)

The room is quiet.

Dust floats in the shafts of morning light, and the air carries a stillness found in places both untouched and waiting.

There on a wooden desk scarred by time and thought, rests a leather-bound book. The cover is worn; the edges curled like pages that have known the weather of hands and years.

But when you open it, the pages inside are blank. All except one.

On the first page, a few lines are written in looping, purposeful script:

This is where your story begins.

There are no instructions, no table of contents—only empty pages stretching out before you. Hundreds of them, untouched and waiting. Each one is blank yet heavy with possibility, as if holding its breath for the story that has yet to be written.

Some who find this book freeze in fear.

"What if I write the wrong thing?"

"What if I waste it?"

"What if I'm not enough?"

Some scribble furiously, their pens racing to keep up with the voices of everyone else—voices that urge them to impress, to prove their worth, to fill the emptiness with noise. Their words scatter across the pages, frantic and uneven, as if speed might silence the doubts that linger in the margins.

Others tear out page after page, crumpling their failed attempts into tiny paper graves before starting over, again and again. And some, worn down by the weight of false starts and unmet expectations, simply close the book halfway through, abandoning it on a shelf, unfinished and forgotten.

But some—some pause.

They trace the ink of that first line with their finger.

They listen. And in the stillness, they hear a whisper. A voice—not from the book, but through it:

Let me show you the adventure I created for you—the story I placed deep within your heart. It is not a tale that demands you perform or prove yourself, but one that invites you simply to follow. It is a story threaded with joy and peace rather than exhaustion, a journey that unveils who you truly are and why you are here. It is the story that opens the door to the place where you were always meant to belong.

Not everyone hears him. Not everyone believes. But those who do feel it like a whisper in their bones. They leave what's safe and predictable and step into the unknown—the story still unfolding.

None of them ever look back with regret. Because what they discover isn't just their story...

... but the One who has been writing it all along.

AFTERWORD

You've just looked through fifty-two keyholes.
Each one gave you a glimpse of what the Kingdom of God is like.
You've also seen how—whether obvious or hidden—Jesus stands
at the center of every one of these stories.

So here's the most important thing I can say in this entire book:

Jesus is the key.
Not a key.
The key.

He is the only one who can unlock the doors to the world you
were made for—a world where you discover the you he created,
the reason you matter, and the place where you're fully known
and wanted

And here's the hard part to hear:
you can't unlock those doors yourself.

It's not because you're not trying hard enough.
It's because you and I aren't qualified.
Only someone who is perfectly holy.
One who is pure in every thought, motive, and action—
could open those doors for us.

That's why Jesus came—
to live the life we could never live.

That's why he died—
to take the penalty for everything we've done wrong.

That's why he rose again—
to defeat death and make a way for us to share in his abundant life, now and forever.

He took on the weight of everything broken in us and everything wrong in the world so he could give us something we could never earn: his life for ours.

Surrender is the price of entry.
But the life on the other side is worth everything.

If you've been peering through these keyholes and wondering what's really behind those doors... he's inviting you to find out.

And you can take that step right now.
All you have to do is ask him.
Offer him your life and accept his in return.

If you take that step, I want to know.
I want to celebrate with you.
I want to be praying for you, specifically.

Send me a message at **Steven@CastMemberChurch.com**.

With much love and hope.

ACKNOWLEDGMENTS

LUCIA—You are the quiet strength behind every page of this book. You've believed in the dreams God placed in me when they felt impossible, carried burdens with me when they felt too heavy, and reminded me, again and again, of who we are with Jesus. Thank you for walking with me into places only faith could lead us, for seeing me when I felt unseen, and for loving me in ways that make the Kingdom feel near. I love you very much.

MARISOL, MIGUEL, AND JUSTIN—You've been my greatest joys and my constant reminders of God's faithfulness. Marisol, your passion, steadfastness, and creativity inspire me more than you know—and Justin, thank you for loving her so well and becoming part of this family with such grace and strength. Miguel, your deep heart and quiet wisdom are gifts I treasure every day. Each of you is a unique reflection of Jesus. To this day, I shake my head in wonder that God has blessed me with you. I am so proud of you, and I love you even more.

JOHNNY DOUGLAS—My dear Northern Irish friend, whose joyful Jesus-likeness has influenced me than you know. You reminded me that God has given me a voice and something worth saying. Your challenge was the genesis of this book. Your laughter, insight, and relentless encouragement have left their mark on every page I have written—and on the person I am becoming.

JIM THACKER—You patiently sifted through my literary clutter, leaving behind words that sound like me—only clearer. Thank you for your gift of turning raw thoughts into something that breathes, and for letting my heart and voice come through. Your friendship means the world to me.

MY DISNEY CAST MEMBER GLOBAL FAMILY—Too many to name, but never too many to hold in my heart. The hundreds of friendships, conversations, dreams, disappointments, hopes, and heartaches we have shared are the reason I tell these stories. I love each and all of you, and I'm deeply blessed to be part of your lives. Keep moving forward.

MOM AND DAD—You've been my cheerleaders from the very beginning—and you still are. For as long as I can remember, your belief in me has been a steady wind at my back, helping me to keep going no matter what lies in front of me.

GORDON MACKENZIE—Your life and words gave me permission to push boundaries and trust the process. You were the gentle nudge toward creative courage. Thank you for showing me how to lean into the unknown with wonder.

RICK RUBEN—Your understanding of authenticity in creativity has been the secret sauce—not just for connecting with the world, but for creating from a place that is true. Thank you for reminding me that what's real will always resonate.

WALT DISNEY—You were a master storyteller, dreamer, and catalyst for so much of what I do. Your courage to imagine—and then create—continues to inspire me to do the same.

JESUS—You are the author of the greatest story ever told. My life overflows with gratitude for the gift of telling stories that point to You. Without You, there would be no meaning, no joy, no peace. Thank You for walking beside me on this journey. May every reader who turns these pages see You, hear You, and feel Your nearness—because this is why I wrote it.

The Kingdom is not confined to pews, pulpits, or programs. It is alive—in conversations, in the laughter and pain of ordinary life. It shows up in the stories we tell, and in the stories we live.

Keyholes has given you glimpses of this Kingdom hidden in plain sight. But the invitation doesn't end here.

KINGDOM iNNOVATORS

Keep moving forward.

Kingdom Innovators is a collective of pioneers, dreamers, and catalysts who long to think beyond the limitations of the modern church. Together with **Cast Member Church**, we are cultivating a global network that reveals Jesus in the most unlikely places—auto repair shops, law offices, exercise classes, movie studio sets, comic book shops, truck stops, karaoke bars, divorce courts, soccer fields, digital spaces, and beyond.

We offer one-to-one and group mentoring online for those ready to step into their calling with courage. We also host **three-day learning laboratories** in Orlando at Walt Disney World and in Disneyland Paris—immersive environments designed to spark fresh imagination and provide practical tools for launching new Kingdom expressions. And if it serves you best, we can come directly to your location and work alongside you and your team, tailoring the experience to your unique context.

This is for the curious. The creative. The restless. The ones who believe faith must be more than ritual, more than religion—who sense it should feel like life itself.

Don't just read the stories. Live them.

Begin your journey at:
CastMemberChurch.com

www.ingramcontent.com/pod-product-compliance
Lightning Source LLC
Chambersburg PA
CBHW050123030726
47505CB00007B/2010